MURDER ON THE FARM

THE PRIVATE INVESTIGATOR ANNIE HUDSON MYSTERY SERIES

BOOK 3

VALERIE BRANDY

EMERALD LION
PRESS

CONTENTS

❀ Created with Vellum

CHAPTER ONE

SOPHIA BARNAK'S corner store was a pleasant enough place— except for the body that lay on the floor.

Private Investigator Annie Hudson stood above the limp form of a man, noting the gash on the back of his head. The wound had resulted in a pool of blood spilling out across the store's original hardwood floors, marring the otherwise immaculate space.

"Charming, isn't it?" Annie said lightly to her partner, FBI Agent Ethan Beckett. His expression informed Annie that clarity was necessary. "The store, not the man," she added, motioning away from the victim on the floor, who didn't seem to take offense at their lack of focus.

"It's cute," Ethan agreed, nodding at the original Coca-Cola posters still decorating the walls, pinned above a jukebox situated in the corner. "In an Americana kind of way. Have you ever seen so many Coca-Cola posters?"

Annie turned, taking in her surroundings. A light-up sign advertising the famous soda hung on the wall, amidst various posters advertising the popular product. Behind the signs, pale, yellow wallpaper depicted a scene of rolling hills and trees growing toward the sky. Annie glanced out an open window at the landscape in the distance that echoed the theme of the wallpaper. The store was situated on a multi-acre farm that backed up to the Dismal Swamp in Virginia's Sunray community, a Polish enclave that had been founded by immigrants many years ago. They had carved the space by hand, and what had started as untamed land was now a pleasant town of well-kept roads and bountiful farms. Sophia Barnak was one of the town's founding residents, and her store had been allowed to remain untouched for many years, standing as a reminder of Sunray's origins. Situated on the edge of a large soybean farm, the corner store prided itself on local goods. Floral, yellow wallpaper covered the space. In the back of the building, a long bar served milkshakes and sodas, and a manual cash register on its surface was prepared to accept payment. Wooden display shelves offered fruits, vegetables, and flowers, all harvested from surrounding farms.

"It's a cozy place," Annie added cheerfully. "Minus what happened to him," she glanced back down at their victim, finally returning her attention to the issue at hand. She bent down examining a discarded shovel that lay by the man's body, its metal edge coated in blood.

"Think we've got a murder weapon," Annie said to Ethan.

"Looks like you two are legit," a husky voice rang out from the store's entryway. In the double doors stood Sheriff Chomski, the only law in town. An impressive mustache framed his features, and a softness in his eyes made Annie like him immediately. "I made some calls," he said, pocketing his radio. "FBI confirmed you're on the case, so— if there's anything I can do..." He didn't finish the sentence but offered a shrug instead. The shrug seemed to suggest he wouldn't be able to do much at all.

"Did you know the victim?" Annie asked, eager to hear from a local.

"Sure did," Sheriff Chomski nodded. "Everybody knew

him. Paul Kaminski was running the farm for the family. Sophia Barnak's relatives live out West. They're her descendants down the line. The had a brother and sister renting the farm, but once they decided to sell, they asked their neighbor Paul to keep the place going. He did right by them and would be still if, you know—"

"Someone didn't bash him over the head?" Ethan offered.

"Exactly," Sheriff Chomski agreed. "Wonder if this'll be a problem for the sale..."

"The property's up for sale?" Annie's ears perked up, her interest in the case growing.

"It's been up for a while," the Sheriff said. "Finally getting interest from what I last heard. Hope this doesn't complicate things for them."

"Hope not," Annie agreed.

"Just out of curiosity," Sheriff Chomski ventured. "We don't get a lotta trouble out here, but when we do, the FBI doesn't usually come calling." The Sheriff paused, evaluating the two outsiders in front of him. "Why this case?" he asked.

Annie smiled. "We made a promise to a friend," she said.

Sheriff Chomski nodded. "Then you're our kind of people," he said. "Around here, everyone's always willing to help a friend."

Annie glanced down at the victim, his body face-down on the wooden floors. "I don't know if he'd agree," she said. She paced in place, then headed for the front doors to the corner store, reaching for a solid master lock that wove between the handles, a chain dangling on one side. "Paul locked the store every night?" she asked.

"That's what the family told me," Sheriff Chomski confirmed. "They let Paul manage the place and he was diligent about makin' sure it was secured."

"And there are no broken windows," Annie added, looking at the few windows that dotted the structure. "Would Paul have brought anyone here who didn't belong?"

Sheriff Chomski let out a low whistle. "No, ma'am. Paul wasn't the social type. Can't see him bringing someone by to a place he didn't own. Would've been outta character."

"Then whoever did this either knew he'd be here or had a key to building." She chewed on the inside of her lip, considering. "Call the family," she said to Sheriff Chomski. "Ask them for a list of everyone who has a key to the corner store."

And with that, her investigation began.

CHAPTER TWO

GLADYS

IT WAS A WARM, summer night when Paul Kaminski was murdered at the corner store, and Gladys had been enjoying it thoroughly. The crickets sang, and a slight breeze made its way through town, wafting past Gladys, who'd been sitting on her porch for the last several hours, doing everything but minding her own business.

Gladys watched as Sheriff Chomski's cruiser pulled up to the edge of Sophia Barnak's corner store, its red and blue lights casting a bright glow across the otherwise abandoned street. She sat in a rocking chair positioned on her wraparound porch, sipping a glass of iced tea, the warm, summer air sticky on her skin. She patted at the sweat pooling on her temples, pushing her short, silver hair behind her ears. In her mid-70s, Gladys was what people around these parts liked to call, "a tough cookie." She'd lived a farm life for as long as she could remember and was the kind of person who always knew what to do in any situation. She could help birth a calf just as well as she could operate a tractor. She wasn't gentle with people, and she didn't expect them to be gentle with her either.

As the closest neighbor to the corner store, Gladys was

uniquely positioned to notice any unique happenings on the property. And this? This was a unique event. Gladys had been sitting on her porch for many hours in a row, which meant she'd seen much of what had happened. She'd heard Paul's scream and watched as a cloaked figure left the property, shrouded in shadow. During the course of the murder, she had sat in place, calmly sipping her iced tea.

In such an instance, Gladys would usually hop on the phone and call the neighborhood contact tree as she always did. Her ancestors had helped settle Sunray, and— as one of the longest-term residents of the area— Gladys knew every- one. In this sense, she was the phone-tree Queen. Last summer, when someone had broken into Gerry's feed barn, Gladys had been the first to mobilize the neighborhood watch. When there was a tornado warning two winters ago, Gladys had put out the word for everyone to head for their basements. Gladys loved to deliver news.

Except, of course, when the news involved her, or when failing to report it would be to her benefit or the benefit of those she was most loyal to. Loyalty was important to Gladys. More important than anything.

Yes— in ordinary circumstances, Gladys wouldn't have waited a single minute to tell the entire community of Sunray what she knew. But these weren't ordinary circumstances. And as soon as she'd heard Paul's shout from the corner store, she'd frozen in place, watching as a second figure walked down the road. It was a figure belonging to a person Gladys knew very well.

It had struck Gladys that she had much to lose or gain in this situation. She'd sat in her chair for hours, waiting for the Police to arrive without saying a single word. She'd watched their squad cars pull up to the corner store, sipping her large iced tea, thinking all the while of a key that was currently dangling on a hook in her foyer closet. It was a simple, bronze key that fit perfectly inside the master lock that secured the doors of the corner store. The family that owned the property had entrusted it to her for emergencies. They hadn't thought twice about it, given Gladys' close proximity to the property and her reputation as an upstanding member of the community.

Now, as if awoken from a trance, Gladys reached into her pocket and removed her cell phone. Instead of calling the phone tree, she entered a single number, still watching those red and blue lights cascade up the street she called home.

She waited for the caller on the other line to answer, then spoke before the person on the other end could even say "hello."

"The FBI is here," she said, a slight tremble in her voice. There was a long pause as she let the weight of it all sink in. On the other end of the line, a deep, male voice answered, his words unintelligible to anyone but Gladys. "I agree," Gladys told him. "They'll be poking around. Think we need to talk about the next steps."

CHAPTER THREE

DR. BURNS

DR. TED BURNS was in his hotel room when he received news of the murder at Sophia Barnak's corner store. Dr. Burns wasn't a "real" Doctor— as his ex-wife so often liked to remind him— but instead held a PhD in American History, with a special emphasis on researching communities that were formed by immigrants. He'd come to Sunray to research its unique place in the history of Polish-American immigrants and was hoping to win a grant from his employer, the University of Virginia, for the study he planned to publish.

But the research wasn't going as well as he'd hoped. Upon his arrival, Dr. Burns had been surprised to find upon his arrival that the community was less than accommodating when they learned an outsider would be, as it was explained to him, "poking around in their business." Dr. Burns had spent many hours gaining the proper clearances to conduct his study, in which Sophia Barnak's corner store was a central focus. But the family back West, along with certain neighbors in the area, protested heavily against his efforts.

He'd made very little headway, and now— it was all about to come crashing down.

Dr. Burns was situated at the small desk in his suite when

the room's landline phone rang. The local bed and breakfast he was staying at offered much in the way of charm. A soft, floral duvet covered the bed, and plush carpets spanned the length of his room, which included a sleeping area, a tiny couch, a desk, a kitchenette, and an attached bathroom. When the landline phone on his desk rang, the sound startled him. He'd only received a handful of calls since arriving in Sunray, and most of them had been from the Inn's proprietor, checking to see if he wanted more towels.

He set aside the essay he was grading and picked up the receiver.

"Hello?" he said.

He waited as the voice on the other line answered in a murmur. "Uh-huh," Dr. Burns acknowledged. He shook his head. "That can't be. I just spoke to Paul the other day. He's been one of only a few residents cooperating with my research..."

Dr. Burn's voice trailed off as the person on the other line interjected.

"Murdered?" Dr. Burns' mouth dropped open. Suddenly, the blood drained from his face, turning his skin a sickly shade of mushroom grey. "No, I'm just as surprised as you are. Of course I'll speak to them," he said, glancing at his briefcase, which was leaning against the wall. He scooted his rolling chair toward it, then rummaged inside, extracting a keychain with a jingle. He sorted through a mess of keys—his rental car fob, the university after-hours electric dongle—landing at an old, bronze key. He slid it between the spiral ring, pulling it off the chain and holding it up in front of him.

"No," he said into the phone receiver, which was crunched between his right ear and his shoulder. "I have no idea why Paul would have been there so late at night."

Dr. Burns grabbed the base of the phone, taking it with him as he made his way to the bedside table. He lifted up the table with his free hand, hiding the key underneath it. The table wobbled just a little, but it seemed to do the job.

"Tomorrow would be great," Dr. Burns added. "They can call me anytime. You too, Sheriff. Have a great night."

With that, he hung up the phone and returned to his desk, surprised at the sweat blistering on his brow. He opened up his laptop and searched for a folder titled "CORNER STORE RESEARCH."

Then, with a simple click and drag, he pulled the entire thing into the trash.

The phone rang, startling him once again. His hand shook as he reached for the receiver.

Tonight, it seemed, was going to be a very long night.

CHAPTER FOUR

VERONICA

VERONICA WAS SITTING in her office at Southern Realty Company when the call about the murder caused her cell phone to buzz. It was late at night— well after hours— and Veronica was the only Real Estate agent still working in the grey, empty building. At twenty-three, she was fresh out of college and still trying to make something of herself.

She flipped her long, black hair over her shoulder, scrolling through a list of leads on her desktop monitor. With each new potential client, an email address had been provided, as well as the person's name and address. Veronica clicked on the next name, then opened up her Outlook inbox and copy/pasted a form letter into a blank email.

"Dear Sir or Madam. Are you still considering selling your home? If so, I would love to help you find your dream property..."

Click. She hit an airplane-shaped icon and the letter whisked off into the digital cloud. Veronica clicked on her "SEND" folder to survey the damage. Tonight alone, she'd sent five-hundred-and- forty-two emails.

And not a single response.

Veronica came from an upper-middle-class life on a farm, where her family had done quite well for themselves. And she was willing to work hard. So it always surprised her when the American dream didn't come knocking. The idea of owning a home with two cars sitting out front wasn't so much what interested Veronica— at least, it wasn't all of it. In Veronica's eyes, the American dream was about security. It was about having the financial dignity to be able to make bold decisions about one's own life. It was the reason her ancestors had left Poland and come to America in the first place. Veronica's parents and grandparents had been successful farmers— they'd created decent lives that way, with finances to be proud of. They hadn't needed degrees to pull themselves by the bootstraps. Instead, they succeeded with just a plot of land, some elbow grease, and determination. Veronica was the first person in her family to break the mold by going to college. She'd assured everyone this was the path to something great. But when she couldn't find a job with her English degree— despite hundreds of applications submitted— Veronica quickly changed gears and applied for her Real Estate license in the hopes of better luck.

Now, she was sitting in front of five hundred unopened emails, wondering how on Earth she would come up with enough money to make her student loan payment this month. But Veronica wasn't one to give up. In a kind of manic frenzy, she clicked right back into the list of leads, copying and pasting the next name into her email draft. Her eyes were open wide, bloodshot and dry, the blue light from the computer screen illuminating her face at a hard, unforgiving angle. She would send as many emails as it took, she assured herself, to accomplish what she intended to do.

Just then, Veronica's cell phone rang. The sound made her jump. She reached for it like it might bite her, hitting the speaker button so the voice on the other end rang out across the room.

"Hello?" She said, curious who could be calling so late at night.

"Sorry to catch you so late," Sherrif Chomski's voice rang out from the other end of the phone. Veronica had met the Sherrif many times because that's the kind of town they lived in— a place where everyone knew each other. "You won't believe this, but there's been a murder at the Sophia Barnak corner store."

Veronica's heart lept into her throat. She swallowed hard. "No," she said into the phone. "That's terrible. I— I can let the family out West know—"

"Already called them," Sheriff Chomski offered. "Don't worry yourself about that. Got another issue I might need your help with..."

Veronica stood as he spoke, grabbing her phone and walking toward the far wall of her office, where a whiteboard sat, a row of command-strip hooks glued to its surface. A handwritten title sat centered above the hooks: VERONICA'S CLIENTS. When Veronica had first started as a Real Estate agent and her passion for the job was fresh, she'd hung the hooks in a moment of optimism, certain that they'd be filled with keys belonging to the many homes she'd represent.

There were a dozen hooks in the row, all of them empty, except for one.

"What's the issue?" Veronica said, staring at the one key that hung on the lone occupied hook. It was a bronze key, old-fashioned and unassuming.

"The FBI has brought in a private detective," the Sheriff's voice answered over the speaker. "She wants to meet with everyone who had a key to the store. Includes you, obviously, since you're representing the sale—"

The sale, Veronica thought ironically. Sophia Barnak's corner store and the attached farmland were Veronica's only active property. In the one year she'd been a realtor, this was her single client. The family back West had only agreed to hire her because they were too far away to know her sales pitch wasn't exactly truthful. When she told them she'd sold one hundred percent of the listings she represented, she'd been careful to leave out that this was only because she'd never represented *any* listings, and zero out of zero was still one hundred percent. Still, she'd given this property her all, and after a few months on the market, an interested party was preparing to make an offer, and the sale of Veronica's dreams was about to become reality.

But a murderer? That could ruin everything.

"Of course," Veronica said into the phone, trying to sound professional. "I'll meet with the Detective anytime. I only hope I can help." Her voice sounded far away, like it was coming out of someone else's mouth.

The pair exchanged some niceties before Veronica hung up, staring at the empty row of hooks on the wall. She reached for the bronze key, taking it off its pedestal and cradling it in her hands, wondering how she'd arrived at such a desperate place.

CHAPTER FIVE
RIGGS

RIGGS WAS at the local watering hole when he heard the news about the murder. The bar was called *"Feisty Mike's,"* and was a staple in Sunray— a dive created in an old barn that had been turned into a community favorite. Music blared from overhead speakers, and straw littered the floor. A mahogany bar spanned the entire length of the barn's shortest wall, and the enormous sliding doors had been left open to allow for indoor-outdoor seating. Behind the bar, multiple TV screens played a re-run of a Football Game.

Riggs stood in the middle of the vast space, nursing an Old Fashioned in a shallow glass, watching the amber liquid swirl clockwise with every sip he took. In between swigs, he would balance the drink on the edge of a pool table, holding his pool-stick over the knuckles of his left hand to get the perfect angle. A man in his late forties, Riggs was proud to say he had a swash-buckling quality about him. His long hair hung down to his shoulders, and a leather belt kept various tools secured around his waist. Combat boots and a tucked-in button-down made him look a bit like Indiana Jones.

Riggs settled into position over the pool table, then took the shot. There was a cracking sound as the eight ball went flying, bumping into another ball and sending it toward a pocket— which it missed, with flair. It rebounded off the edge of the pocket and slid across the table, ending up in a spot of no strategic importance. Across the table, Riggs's opponent smirked, pulling at the edge of his beard.

"You've gotten worse at pool since we came to Sunray," Riggs's opponent, Seth, smiled. "Better hope we find the prize, otherwise you won't be able to pay me all your lost bets."

"Ten bucks a game was always too steep for me and you know it," Riggs smiled back. Seth was Riggs' business partner, and the two of them had traveled around the world together, finding treasure in the strangest of places. So far, their greatest gets included a sunken pirate ship dating back to the 1600s, some illegal Egyptian artifacts hidden in the walls of a house in Canada, and countless smaller wins across the globe. In the world of treasure-hunting Riggs and Seth were small-time operatives. But they still made enough money to support a nomad lifestyle that took them across the world, from South America to Europe. Their two-bedroom portable command station of an RV was parked outside, storing metal detectors, old maps, and a LIDAR system that allowed them to look through layers of Earth using radio frequencies. Together, Riggs and Seth had seen the world.

But Sunray? Sunray was special. To Riggs, at least. In the few months he'd been here, Riggs had found something that had eluded him in his travels across the world. There was something unique about this place. It made a person feel at home. For the first time, Riggs was wondering what it would feel like to stay in one place. What it would mean to live in a town where all the neighbors knew each other, and there was no danger to be had. Sunray was that kind of place.

Riggs was lining up to take the next shot when a local resident waved at him from the bar. Riggs recognized the man as the owner of a pharmacy just down the street. He approached their pool table, already speaking before he was even in earshot.

"The farm and corner store!" The man shouted at them. "Did you hear?"

Riggs set down his pool stick. Surely the man couldn't be talking about *the* corner store— which was situated on the very farm on which he'd been looking for a certain type of treasure.

"Not Sophia Barnak's corner store?" Riggs said, suddenly alarmed. "It didn't burn down or—"

"No," the man waved a hand. "Someone was murdered there."

Riggs inhaled sharply. He'd spent many hours on the property, analyzing the soil quality and digging in the dirt. At the owning family's request, Riggs had been called into town to solve a mystery dating back to the early 1900s.

When Sophia Barnak arrived to the farm from Poland, she'd claimed to bring many treasures with her. And, when she died, she told the entire town that she'd buried those treasures somewhere on the farm. Hidden in those acres, if Sophia Barnak was to be believed, was something precious and valuable.

"Someone was murdered?" Riggs repeated dumbly.

The local man nodded. "They want to talk to anyone who had a key."

Riggs reached into his pocket, letting his fingers close around a keychain. There, his hands brushed the ridge of an old, bronze key that had been given to him by the landowners, who had hoped he could solve the mystery of the treasure before the impending sale.

"Everyone?" Riggs asked. He offered a pointed glance at Seth, both of them sure that their job here in Sunray had just become infinitely more complicated.

CHAPTER SIX

KAREN

KAREN KAMINSKI WAS at home when she heard about her husband Paul's murder. It had happened in such a blur that even several hours later, Karen sat alone on the edge of her bed, trying to recount everything that had occurred.

When Sheriff Chomski had knocked on her front door, Karen had assumed the local high school boys had once again stolen the school's mascot and hidden it in the Soybean fields behind her house. It wasn't until Sheriff Chomski delivered the news about Paul's demise that Karen suddenly realized her life had changed forever.

She remembered grabbing her coat off a hook near the door, her legs carrying her outside toward the Sheriff's waiting squad car. They'd driven the corner store in silence, and Karen had stared out the window, thinking about her marriage to Paul, and all the ways she wished it had been different. When the squad car's tires had pulled up to the property's edge, Karen had wondered at how little time she'd spent in a place that had been a Sunray staple for so long.

Sheriff Chomski had let her into the corner store, its doors wide open and unlocked, crime scene tape and a couple of officers protecting the scene. Karen entered, looking past the rows of products, her eyes landing on her husband's limp form, a pool of blood around his head.

"Someone struck him," Sheriff Chomski offered. "The display case is tipped over and we think there was a struggle. We've brought in a Private Investigator. One of the best, I'm told. She wants to speak with everyone who had a key to the building, which would include you. I'll be reaching out later, of course, once you've had a chance to process—"

His words became one long, monotone sound as Karen focused on what was in front of her:

A fresh start.

Karen had attempted to fight the feeling of peace that rose in her chest, but she couldn't. She'd waited until Sheriff Chomski had dropped her safely at home to let herself exhale. She'd wandered into the kitchen, reaching into the cabinets and grabbing a stack of identical coffee mugs, which she threw into the trash one at a time. She'd watched as their pieces broke apart, each one making a delightful shattering noise.

They were Paul's favorite mugs, and now they were nothing but a shattered mess inside the kitchen trashcan. Later, Karen took a warm bubble bath and snuggled into bed, stretching out over the entirety of the mattress.

Now, she was lying flat on her back, staring at the ceiling, thinking about what new coffee mugs she might buy. Perhaps she'd get mugs in all different colors, no two the same, each with its own different pattern or design. She looked forward to interjecting some whimsy— some adventure— into her life.

Karen would never admit it out loud, but the truth was: She was relieved her husband was dead.

———

The next morning, Karen Kaminski had awoken in a panic. She'd sat straight up in bed, a horrible realization hitting her.

She'd been so lost thinking about her newfound freedom that she'd forgotten to look out for someone else— someone most important to her.

She'd dressed with urgency, grabbing her car keys and running to her pickup truck, stuck by the importance of what she needed to achieve. She drove herself straight to the Sheriff station, and now, she was standing outside, hoping she could make a deal.

She wrapped her cardigan tighter around her shoulders and knocked three times. The door opened with a squeal. Sheriff Chomski stood in front of her, holding a styrofoam cup filled with tea. He was the only person on duty this early in the morning, and haggard gray hair sprouting from his beard implied this was a frequent occurrence.

"Karen," he said, his eyes large. "Thought you'd be home, after everything that happened. Wouldn't surprise me if you wanted to lay in bed for a week, what with Paul being gone—"

"I'm not here for Paul," she said, her voice strong. "I'm here because I need a favor."

"Alright," Sheriff Chosmki hesitated, not sure if he should agree before finding out what the favor was. "You know I'm always here for you—"

"Not from the Sheriff," Karen said, flipping her hair behind one shoulder. "I need a favor from my friend from kindergarten. You remember when I fell off the slide and scraped my knee? You helped me walk to the nurse's station."

"I did," Sheriff Chomski agreed. He encountered this problem often working in the same town he'd lived in all his life. It was difficult to insist on law and order when everyone in town remembered you as a gangly teenager.

"You and I know this place. We know what it means. Those detectives you brought in—"

"Annie and Ethan."

"Well they don't understand our ways like we do. They're

'gonna try to make something there that wasn't soon as they see the report."

"The fight between you and Paul?" Sheriff Chomski sighed. "That was years ago. They won't think anything of it. A domestic dispute doesn't automatically lead to murder accusations."

"Not that one," Karen shook her head. "The other one. At the bar, a week ago. The fight between Paul and Riggs."

Sheriff Chomski's eyebrows raised in surprise. "That was just Paul bein' drunk," he said. "They won't pay it any mind."

"I want it erased," Karen answered.

"Why?"

There was a long pause in which Karen considered how to answer.

"Are you worried about Paul's legacy?" Sheriff Chomski continued. "Don't be. Everyone around here knew Paul was a hard-working man with a few flaws, one of them being a love of whiskey. If that report comes out it won't matter one bit. Unless Gladys gets ahold of it and then—"

"Not Paul," Karen said. "It's not Paul I'm worried about."

Sheriff Chomski looked her up and down, suddenly understanding why she'd come to see him.

"Outsiders aren't always treated kindly," Karen said. "What happened that night— it was my fault. I don't want someone implicated in a crime they didn't commit because of a choice I made."

Sheriff Chomski nodded. His loyalty to the law was his fourth most sacred commitment. His third was his commitment to Sunray. His second was his commitment to his family. And his first was his commitment to God.

He'd known Karen since they were children. And if she'd gotten herself in trouble, it seemed like the right thing to do was to help her get out of it. She was his neighbor and his childhood friend.

"I'll make it disappear," he said. "Come on in. You look like you could use a cup of coffee." He ushered her into the Sheriff's office, not sure he'd done the right thing, but satisfied that he'd stayed loyal to what mattered most. "Stacey's comin' by later. Are you still teaching sculpture classes? She could use a lesson. Wants to be a Sheriff like me but I'm tryin' to point her toward anything else. I'd even settle for the arts at this point."

"For you?" Karen smiled. "As many lessons as you need." The door shut softly behind them.

CHAPTER SEVEN

"THIS IS WHERE YOUR SOURCE LIVES?" Ethan asked Annie, motioning to a cluster of vining plants in front of him. They were rooted in the Earth so close together that their twining limbs— which featured bright, red, flowers— seemed to tangle over one another, making a mess of the trellising upon which they grew. The trellising was leaning up against the exterior wall of a small tool shed, its doors wide open. Inside, trowels and buckets hung from the walls, and packages of fertilizer sat on the floor. "Is he a hummingbird?"

"He has his own ways," Annie shrugged. She examined the vines and the trellising, shrugging her shoulders at the strangeness of it all. "Honestly, I think he could use some help. He's made the entrance too obvious."

"The entrance?" Ethan asked. "Entrance to what?" He glanced around the trellising, which sat on an otherwise empty patch of land. The farm looked barren this time of year, given that the upcoming crops were nothing but seeds in the ground. This land was entirely empty, with the exception of the tool shed, and an old house far off in the distance.

"Strange to put the tool shed so far from the house, isn't it?" Annie stated. She bent closer to the trellising, running her fingers across the vines. "Shall we?" she asked. Without another word, she pulled hard on the vines, and the trellising swung open, revealing a secret door. Hinges dotted the left-hand side, buried under the vines, which groaned under the pressure, but— judging by the creases in their tender limbs— the plants seemed used to the intrusion.

Ethan peaked through the door, revealing a set of stairs within the storage shed, descending down into the Earth. "But I checked the shed!" Ethan exclaimed. He returned to the shed's open doors to verify, finding nothing on the back wall but hanging tools. Annie joined him, knocking on the wall so that a hollow noise echoed. "It's a false wall," she explained. "The stairs on the other side. And the entrance is—"

"Through the exterior trellising," Ethan shook his head. "I know guys like this. Don't tell me he's a doomsdayer."

"I wouldn't say that. I'd simply say he's incredibly prepared," Annie smiled, stepping out of the shed and back towards the newly revealed entrance in the trellising.

"Does he know we're coming?"

"The thing about Milo," Annie assured him, "Is that he tends to know everything. And that's how he's going to help us."

With that, she made her way down the stairs, disappearing into the darkness with Ethan two steps behind her.

"You closed the trellis behind you, right?" Milo asked, pushing his dark hair out of his eyes. At twenty-five years old, Milo was still navigating the awkwardness of his youth and the independence of adulthood. His bowl haircut hung low over his glasses, his skin pale, his frame wiry. He was seated in front of a computer, unbothered by the cement walls of the bunker that surrounded him.

"We did," Ethan assured him, looking around the space. "You know, for a bunker, this is actually pretty—"

"Nice?" Milo offered. "Yeah, when I graduated my parents let me turn this place into my own little fortress. They think I'm crazy, but when the next Civil War breaks out, I'll be ready."

"It's lovely," Annie smiled at him, glancing around the space. The bunker had been converted into its own basement apartment. A full kitchen with top and bottom cabinets and impressive tiling was situated in the far corner. It faced an open-concept living room, a soft corduroy couch positioned in front of an enormous flat-screen TV.

At the other end of the bunker, Ethan flicked a light switch on, peeking into the open door of a master bedroom with an attached bath. "Pretty nice for a survival shelter," Ethan agreed. "What made you decide to, you know— renovate?"

"Have you seen rental prices these days?" Milo asked. "Better to reconfigure my own space and work with what I got. Plus, I'm safer here than anywhere." He pointed upward at the steel ceiling. "Government can't track my signal as easily. You know the NSA listens to everything. Not just on the phone, but through the internet. But I'm always one step ahead of the alphabet agencies…" Milo paused as if he'd made a grave error, then turned to Annie. "You said he's cool, right?"

"Ethan's cool," Annie agreed. "He's in the FBI but he wants to find out who the Real Estate Ripper is as badly as I do."

Milo nodded. "I can help you," he said. "But you've gotta give Sheriff Chomski some assistance on the Paul Kaminski case. It was good luck you happened to be out here already—"

"Why do you care about the Kaminski case?" Ethan asked, curious.

"Not me," Milo shook his head. "My girlfriend Stacey is the Sheriff's daughter. The thing about Sheriff Chomski is, well, he gets real spun up when something happens that's outside his wheelhouse. She's worried about it, and if it's her problem, it's my problem." Milo spun around in his computer chair, a fidget spinner circling his finger. "Plus, I want to see the community safe. If there's a killer on the loose, I want 'em caught. The thing about living in a place like this is that we stick together."

"We've spoken to the Sheriff," Annie confirmed. "We'll find out who killed Paul Kaminski. But in exchange, I need you to do something neither Ethan nor I can do ourselves."

"Happy to," Milo said, motioning at the bank of screens in front of him. A dozen monitors were affixed to the wall, littered with computer coding and proxy website hubs. "What do you need? Information on a suspect? Names, addresses?"

Annie reached into her briefcase and pulled out a manilla envelope, handing it to Milo. He opened it, extracting a list of IP addresses.

"The person who killed my brother and took Ethan's sister recently reached out to me to pull me into an investigation. They knew a murder had been committed, and wrote a letter that was sent to me via courier to make me take the case. The problem is, the letter arrived just a few hours after the murder. Which means they accessed the case via Police Servers. Our friend ran a check and found the case information was accessed by one of these IP addresses in the time between the murder, and when the letter was sent. It's a four-state radius. I need to know everything about those IPs."

"Could take a while," Milo nodded. "The problem is that each IP address is connected to a specific computer, and we can't know how many people accessed it without some serious research. I'm talking security cameras, key tracing..."

"All of it," Annie agreed. "I want to know every single person that could have accessed those computers on the list."

"I'll have to go through the NSA's backdoor," Milo

muttered aloud. "They're the only ones that have this kind of access. Phone calls. Voicemails. Emails."

"I'm not hearing any of this," Ethan said, a pained look on his face. He pretended to examine a wall of freeze-dried survival food, busying himself with reading the labels on the back of the packages.

"If the FBI can do a better job, let them," Milo smiled at him. "Oh, but wait, you need a *warrant*—"

"Because that's the law!" Ethan countered.

"Bro," Milo ran a hand through his hair. "Don't you get it? The law only works one way: it's about what a person can get away with, and what they can't." He leaned in, gripping the edges of his chair. "The law says private citizens aren't supposed to be spied on by the government, and yet the NSA exists. What's the law except rules from people in power?"

"That's different," Ethan said, jaw clenched.

"Why?" Milo shrugged.

"Because they're the good guys. We're the good guys."

Milo laughed. "Yeah," he said, waving the papers he held in the air. "So good you're looking for a serial killer who's likely also a Police Officer. Sorry, bro, but it's not the uniform that makes someone good or bad."

"You have to keep it quiet," Annie interjected, trying to de-escalate the moment. "No one can know we're poking around."

"Quiet is my middle name," Milo smiled. "It's this guy you've gotta worry about," he nodded at Ethan, then leaned in, whispering to Annie. "He's got 'snitch' written all over him."

"I agree," Annie laughed, taking in Ethan's irate expression. "But he's my snitch." And with that, she led Ethan by the hand back up the stairs, hoping coffee and a cheeseburger would bring him back to life.

CHAPTER EIGHT

THE SHERIFF'S station in Sunray was an outpost of Chesapeake County's larger hub. The two-room building's exterior was original to the settlement and hadn't changed much in over one hundred years. Wooden pillars held up the awning, and the stone walls were marked by erosion due to weather. Inside the building, the station was quaint and welcoming.

"It's a two-person job around here," Sheriff Chomski said to Annie and Ethan, nodding across the room at his partner, Cadet Stacey Chomski. Stacey was barely twenty-three, and— as an officer in training— spent most of her time monitoring the front desk and pushing paper around. "Stacey gets it done," the Sheriff smiled.

"I'm his daughter so he has to say that," Stacey answered. "I set you guys up in Dad's office. He said he can live without it for a few weeks and tolerate working out here in the bullpen with me."

She led Annie and Ethan into the only other room in the building. It was a tidy space with a desk in the center and two chairs on the opposite side. Photos of Sheriff Chomski, his wife, and Stacey hung on the walls, along with an undergraduate degree and a framed baseball bat with an athlete's signature marking the side.

"Did Milo tell you how important this is?" Stacey whispered as she shut the door.

"He did," Annie agreed.

"And Dad doesn't know I asked for you, right?"

"We said the FBI sent us," Ethan answered. "Which is true, to some degree. They've given me the okay to assist on this case given that it connects to a larger," he paused, searching for the right word, "... *problem* we're tracking."

"Good," Stacey breathed a sigh of relief. "The thing is, crimes around here usually involve the local high school or a traffic accident. We've only had a couple of serious situations as long as I've been alive." She sat in her Dad's office chair, crossing her legs to her chest. "And the last one... it was a murder of a homeless guy that was just crossing through. My Dad nearly lost it trying to solve the thing. He drove my Mom crazy. Made himself sick. That was a decade ago and I was just a kid, but I still remember how bad it was. I don't ever want to see that happen to him again."

"We'll get to the bottom of it so your Dad doesn't have to," Annie said. "Don't worry."

"I think he's relieved you're here," Stacey said. "It doesn't even seem to bother him that you're taking the lead. After last time— maybe he feels the same way I do."

"Could be," Ethan agreed.

"Still, he's not Milo's biggest fan," Stacey blushed when mentioning her boyfriend. "He says he's a hoodlum and an anarchist and a rule-breaker. I tell him only two of those are true but I won't say which two." Stacey laughed.

"Milo has his own way of doing things, that's for sure," Annie agreed.

Stacey opened up a drawer in the desk, pulling out a stack of files. "I got these for you," she said, passing the files to Annie. "My Dad said you wanted to speak to everyone who had access to the corner store. He called the family out West and got the name of every single person who has a key. We ran a background check on everyone and then, when Dad wasn't looking... I had Milo dig a little *deeper* if you know what I mean. He'll email you everything he finds."

"Helpful," Annie agreed. "Thank you so much."

"Sure," Stacey brightened and stood, sensing that her guests wanted time to themselves. "You let us know if you need anything. And thank you, again." With that, she let herself out, closing the door behind her with a soft click.

"Not a bad room to work from," Ethan looked around the space, admiring the pictures hanging on the wall. "I could get used to this myself."

"I thought farm life wasn't for you?" Annie smiled.

"I thought so too, but I understand what Stacey means. The more you see, the more it builds up. And it's got nowhere to go, so you just shove it aside, and then you have all these boxes inside your mind that you can't empty out. Maybe Sherriff Chomski just needs some time to empty it all out. Poor guy *does* seem relieved we're here."

"And?" Annie asked.

"And maybe he's got the right idea. About life. Maybe after we figure out who the Real Estate Ripper is and we see him locked up—"

"What?"

"Maybe we find a small town. Help keep the people there safe. And drink iced tea on a porch."

"Who are you and what have you done with Ethan Beckett?" Annie smiled.

"You don't want to drink iced tea with me?"

"Depends on the porch."

Annie opened the files, finding a photo in each one, along with various and sundry information about each person. She removed the pictures one by one, digging in the desk for a collection of pins and hanging them on a corkboard across the room.

"You're not entertaining my idea?" Ethan asked, unable to keep himself from taking an opportunity to tease Annie.

"Quite the opposite," Annie answered. "I'm trying to get you one step closer to that porch. We can rest when we're done." She motioned at the photos on the board. "Our suspects," she said. "Five people had access to the corner store. It goes without saying it's also possible they lent their keys to someone else, or that Paul brought someone with him that night. At this time, these are our leads, but we must be open-minded to other possibilities that present themselves."

"Noted," Ethan said.

"First up," Annie continued, reading from the first file. "We have Gladys. She's a neighbor and her property butts up to the corner store. The family out West stated that they gave her a copy of the key to be used in emergencies only."

"You'd think this would qualify," Ethan said. "Has she heard about the murderer?"

"She claims she didn't hear or see anything until the Sherriff arrived," Annie said. "Next up, we have Dr. Ted Burns."

She pointed to the second picture on the board, which featured a distinct-looking man in a suit, his spectacle-laden eyes looking back out at them. "Dr. Burns is a researcher from the University of Virginia. Much to the family's chagrin, he's gathering information to provide to the historical society given Sunray's unique position as an American Colony built by Polish Immigrants."

"The family's unhappy with the research?"

"Yes," Annie said, reading from the file.

"But they gave him a key anyway?"

"It appears there was a push from the surrounding community to allow Dr. Burns access. The Sophia Barnak Corner Store was the first commercial building constructed in town and played a central part in Sunray's development along with the original church and school building. The family wanted to honor the wishes of the community, so they finally relented and gave Dr. Burns access."

"Checks out," Ethan said. "I'd do the same. Better to get along with your neighbors."

"Especially in a small community," Annie agreed. "Next, we have the realtor, Veronica." Annie pointed at the third photo on the board, which showed Veronica in a blouse, arms crossed, smiling. "She's young. Hungry. Just joined Southern Realty. The family allowed her to list the property after receiving a cold call. She'd been soliciting different landowners in the area to see if they wanted to sell, and it just so happened the family out West had already been thinking of listing the property."

"You take a million shots, at least one's gotta pay off," Ethan agreed. "Has she sold it?"

"It's been up for six months with no traction, but they finally have an offer in the works," Annie answered. "She has a key to access the corner store in order to show potential buyers the space."

"And who's this looker?" Ethan nodded at the fourth image in the row— a photo of Riggs on a dig site, covered in mud.

"Name is Riggs," Annie read from the next file. "He's a treasure- hunter. He moves from place to place, looking for valuable artifacts from different historical periods and lives off the funds from what he finds. Some of his ethics have been called into question, but he's legitimate." She reached into the file and held up a print-out of a magazine article chronicling Riggs' endeavors. "In the article, they call him an antiquities pirate."

"Why's he here?" Ethan asked. "There's no antiquities in Sunray. America's too new."

"It seems like he hasn't had a big win in a while," Annie said, reviewing his file. "He's moved onto smaller projects to keep the money flowing. Colonial antiques. Indigenous arti-facts. I get the impression he blew through his money from digs abroad. He's land-locked, stuck in North America until he can get his funds moving again."

"What's he looking for?"

"The family states Sophia Barnak said upon her death that she had buried something on the property. She claimed it was something of great value, and she'd hidden it on the farm where no one would find it. For years after her death, neigh-bors came digging, shovels out at night."

"Nice neighbors," Ethan laughed. "Interesting our victim was hit with a shovel, isn't it?"

"It is," Annie agreed. "In thirty years, nobody's found a thing. But the family is allowing Riggs to check the property before the sale goes through. For peace of mind. You know, just—"

"— just in case? Can't blame them. I'd do the same. It'd be a shame to sell the place before finding the treasure."

"Once the idea of a hidden treasure is in your mind— once the question has been introduced— it's a difficult concept to shake, isn't it?" Annie agreed. "Even if you never found one piece of it, a person would always wonder." She reached for the next file, glancing up at the final picture on the board. The photograph was a charming image of a woman in her late '50s with dark hair and looked to be taken from a newspaper clip-ping. It showed her standing in front of an old farmhouse, an enormous sculpture of a winged angel by her side. "Last up, we have Karen Kaminski. Paul Kaminski's wife. She had access to a key to the corner store given that Paul was tending to the property. They were married for thirty years. They're both from this area. Appears they knew each other as children and their families were close."

"Any indication as to whether or not the marriage was a happy one?" Ethan asked.

"No, but I'm sure we can find out as much when we go to

speak with her," Annie smiled. "Apparently she won sculpture of the year at the local arts fair. She's quite the artist. Her biography states she sold some pieces here and there, even had a few in galleries."

"Sculpture is a rare talent for someone who turns out to be a murderer," Ethan pondered. "I've found most artists to be the peaceful type."

"That's an excellent suspicion," Annie answered. "But we'll wait until we ascertain the facts."

"Who do you want to interview first?"

"I'll start with the one who's behaving most out of character, based on what we know about them," Annie said, walking toward the board and pulling down a single photograph. Gladys' face shined back at her, a pair of pearl earrings dotting her quaint little ears.

"Looks like a nice lady," Ethan said.

"Don't they always?" Annie answered. "It's the nice ones you have to look out for."

"That sounds a lot like a suspicion to me."

Annie smiled to herself. She was the type to delight in her own hypocrisy, and although she would never admit it out loud, Annie loved that her suspicions so often led to facts.

"Let's set up a meeting."

CHAPTER NINE

GLADYS

GLADYS' living room was a carpeted cavern. Heavy drapes blocked enormous windows, shutting out the light. Striped, pink wallpaper coated the surface of every corner. Overhead, antique light fixtures dripped dangerously toward the floor, their glass droplets dusty from lack of attention.

"Paul was such a pillar of the community," Gladys said. She was seated at the Queen Anne table in the dining section of the living room, a teapot in her hand. "Much like me, he's what we call a lifer. Born here. Raised here. He knew Sunray better than anyone. This place was a part of him— and he was a part of it." Gladys tipped over the teapot, pouring amber liquid into two teacups positioned in front of her guests— Annie and Ethan. They sat across from her at the table, hands politely folded in their laps.

"You know Paul well, then?" Annie said, raising the cup to her lips and forcing herself to take a sip. She had noticed the teacups were coated in dust but forced herself to be polite and engage in a drink. Ethan watched as Annie choked down her tea, resisting the urge to laugh.

"Very well," Gladys confirmed. "We were more than just neighbors. We grew up together. Our parents were friends, and we went to the same elementary school. That's a special thing about Sunray. Family legacy. Our ancestors grew up together, and so did we." Gladys stood, walking toward the curtains that obscured a window and pushing them open, the scent of days gone by clinging to the air. "Look out that way," she nodded at the open farmland in front of her. It was only dirt today, but rivets in the ground indicated seeds had been planted. The promise of future bounty sizzled in the soil. "You're in the middle of the triad of original farmland. My property. Paul's property. And the Sophia Barnak corner store. Our three lots were the first settled by Polish immigrants. Our ancestors came with nothing, and they built this place. Over time, some of the lots have shifted, but we all try to keep ownership in the family. These three..." she pointed out the window into the distance, where the corner store was visible, "These three lots have stayed in the same families for generations."

"Until now," Annie said, clearing her throat. When Gladys didn't answer, she offered clarity. "Because of the sale. The family back West is selling the property. You knew, of course?"

Gladys took a seat again, sighing heavily. "There's not much that goes on around here I *don't* know," she said. "We tried to convince them not to sell, but they were set on the idea. For years, they'd been renting the land."

"Renting it to who?" Annie asked, suddenly very curious.

"A brother and sister pair. They grew up out here and were farming the land, but decided to move. That's when the family went on about the sale."

"But you'd prefer they hadn't?" Annie probed.

Gladys threw her hands in the air as if to say she meant well, but was entitled to her opinions. "It's none of my business," Gladys said, giving Annie the distinct impression this was something she said quite often, "But it's generally preferred around here that land is kept in the family. It's a

Polish tradition. You break the land into smaller pieces and leave it to your children or nearest relative. Selling it, well, I don't have to tell you. It changes the community."

"Are there others who feel the same way?" Annie asked.

"Of course," Gladys shrugged.

"You would know, I suppose," Annie pressed. "I've heard you're well-connected here. I believe you were described to me as the heart of the town."

Gladys blushed, and Ethan shook his head. He had most definitely *not* heard Gladys described as the heart of the town. In fact, he distinctly remembered Sheriff Chomski's daughter telling Annie Gladys was the asshole of the town. But Annie liked to embellish when it suited her objectives.

"That's flattering," Gladys agreed. "But it's simply that I've lived here the longest. There's not a single person I don't know."

"Did you know Sophia Barnak?" Annie asked.

Gladys nodded. "I was in my prime when she was in her later years, running the store. She would always give me a coke or a milkshake, on the house, because she'd known me since I was a child. She was a shrewd businesswoman. Knew how to keep the community happy."

"And what do you make of these rumors of treasure?" Annie added. "She's been gone for thirty years. If she'd really hidden treasure on the farm, wouldn't it have been found by now?"

"Nonsense," Gladys took a sip of her tea. "Sophie likely made the whole thing up just to drive the town crazy. Her own private joke, if you will."

"Why would she do that?" Annie wondered.

Gladys leaned in. "Do either of you have siblings?" Neither Annie nor Ethan answered, but both of them bristled. They'd lost their siblings years ago in a crime that remained unsolved, and it wasn't an easy thing to discuss. Especially not with suspects in their investigations. Thankfully, Gladys covered the silence. "Well when you have a sibling, you love them. You'd die for them. But you also like to read their diary, tease them about their crush, and tell them when they look stupid in their favorite jacket. Sophie's relationship with Sunray was kind of like that. She loved the place. Would've done anything for it. But given the opportunity to set the whole town searching for treasure on a wild goose chase, who wouldn't decide to have a little fun?"

"Surprisingly, I know exactly what you mean," Annie agreed. "Just a couple more questions..." Annie pretended to glance at a notebook by her side. Even though she had a photographic memory and knew exactly what she planned to ask next, Annie found it comforted a suspect when she pretended to be less astute. "The family back West gave you a key. Why was that?"

"They liked to know they had someone around in case of emergencies. I'm a neighbor and a trusted member of the community. I supposed they felt I'd be on call in case of a fire, or other problem on the grounds."

"They had Paul for that though, didn't they?" Annie said.

"Yes, but on the off chance he couldn't be reached, I was their backup contact," Gladys said.

"But why you?" Annie pressed. "They could have picked anyone. There's a neighbor on the other side..."

"But of *course* they would pick me!" Gladys exclaimed, trying not to show her frustration. "I'm head of neighborhood watch, in fact. I have the entire community phone tree at my disposal. It's a clear and obvious selection. They intentionally chose me for the job."

"What were you doing the night of Paul's murder?" Annie switched gears.

"I—" Gladys stammered. "I was sitting on the porch enjoying an iced tea."

"The porch that has a perfect view of the corner store?" Annie asked, going in for the kill.

"Well, yes—" Gladys answered.

"Did you hear anything at the time of the murder?"

"No, but I was also reading—"

"Did you see anyone leave the property, or any cars parked outside?"

"It was quite dark," Gladys countered. "I don't know if you noticed but we don't have street-lamps on this road. I've been petitioning for quite some time to have them put in—"

"Did you call anyone on the neighborhood watch list when the police arrived?"

"I— well, I didn't think to—"

"Surely you would have activated the phone tree as soon as you realized a crime had been committed. Your file actually shows you've activated the phone tree a dozen times in the past year. You're quite on top of things, typically."

"Well, I…" Gladys searched for an answer but none came. "I didn't want to be intrusive," Gladys said, finally settling on what she believed to be the most plausible explanation for her behavior. "I saw Sheriff Chomski arriving and when the crime scene tape came out, I knew something terrible had happened. I didn't want to alert the phone tree until I was sure it would be helpful. When I spoke to the Sheriff later in the evening, he assured me there was no need to call anyone. He said he had it under control. I do have the list, though, if you'd like it," she added helpfully. "Maybe somebody saw something. A few of them live on this road."

"That would be so helpful, thank you," Annie answered. "We'll take the list and then be on our way."

Gladys stood, retrieving a copy of the neighborhood watch list from her office and handing it to Annie with a sick feeling in her stomach. As she walked her guests to the door, she was struck by the sense that she'd made a mistake not calling that evening.

"I really didn't want to alarm anyone or get in the way of the investigation," Gladys added as she opened the front door for Annie and Ethan. "Paul was a dear friend. If I'd done anything that interfered with finding whoever did this to him, well— I'd never forgive myself."

"Don't worry," Annie said, nodding. She touched Gladys' arm with the gentlest sympathy. "There is absolutely nothing you could have done then, and nothing you *could* do now, that would keep me from finding out who killed Paul Kaminski. I promise you that."

With those final words, Annie and Ethan made their way down the steps of the front porch, strolling toward the rental car they'd parked down the road. Gladys felt a shiver run down her spine, and couldn't shake the feeling that she'd made a very, *very* big mistake.

CHAPTER TEN

DR. BURNS

DR. BURNS TAPPED his knee anxiously. He was sitting on the couch in the lobby of the small Bed & Breakfast he'd begun to call home during his research trip here in Sunray. The lobby was a quaint, charming space that gave the impression of a library. Couches were scattered throughout to allow guests the opportunity to lounge in their own corner, and tall bookshelves lined the walls, the pine wood shelves filled with tomes of all different genres. A check-in desk sat at the back of the room, and coffee tables littered the sitting areas. A continental breakfast had been laid out with an assortment of pastries, with a Keurig nearby.

"It's a fascinating place," Dr. Burns said to his guests. Annie and Ethan were seated across from him on a plush, cream couch, enjoying two croissants on paper plates. "Sunray, I mean. It's a pocket of American history that so often goes overlooked. Everyone likes to research colonial settlers, but the waves of immigrants that came in the early 1900s offer a unique story about our history."

"That's your area of expertise, then?" Annie asked.

"Yes," Dr. Burns confirmed. "My PhD is in American History, so I'm equipped to research any time period. But I specialize in later waves of immigration, long after the original colonists."

"I'm sorry," Ethan interjected. "But I didn't catch— what University do you work for?"

"The University of Virginia," Dr. Burns said proudly, adjusting his tie. "Our United States History Program is one of the best in the country."

"And what made Sunray appeal to you?" Annie questioned. "I mean, there's so many places you could have gone. So many distinct waves of immigrants. Italian communities. Irish communities. Was it the Polish history, or something specific about this area?"

Dr. Burns took a sip of his coffee as he considered his answer. "Well, I happen to have a bit of Polish ancestry myself," he offered. "But it wasn't that so much as the unique way this community has stayed intact. There's people living here— today— who can trace their ancestry all the way back to the original founders."

"And what was the role of Sophia Barnak's corner store in all of this?" Annie hedged. "I hope you don't mind, but Sheriff Chomski informed us you're one of a handful of people that have a key in your possession."

Dr. Burns sighed, leaning back on the couch to stretch his legs. "The research doesn't hold water without the corner store. Do you know anything about the way academia works?"

"We don't," Ethan offered.

"I have to justify everything I do," Dr. Burns said, scratching at his facial hair. "My research is funded by grants with escalating landmarks, and at each point, I have to reapply and prove I've delivered on previous promises to reach the next funding level."

"Your salary alone doesn't support the research?" Annie asked.

"Oh, of course it does!" Dr. Burns said, a little too enthusiastically. "No problems there. It's just a church-and-state situation. The University prefers we rely on grant funding for research expenses, which isn't an issue as far as I'm concerned. However, securing grants is rather political and I face challenges given that I have a unique way of looking at things."

"So why the corner store?"

"It supports my thesis," Dr. Burns said. "My research is about the geographical formation of community through strategic alignment of key resources within planning the layout of a town in the settlements of first-generation immigrants."

"Huh?" Ethan said.

Dr. Burns leaned in, his eyes lighting up at the opportunity to explain his research. He reached for a salt shaker on the table, then a pepper shaker, and finally— a napkin.

"I want you to imagine you've just moved to a new country. You don't know the language. You don't know the laws. But you've been given a plot of land, along with ten other immigrants who share your values and culture. Together, you start from scratch. How do you build a town that meets your needs? What are the things a settlement requires?"

"A hospital," Ethan said.

"Not back in the day," Dr. Burns answered. "The first thing you'd build... was a church."

He put down the salt shaker, indicating it would serve as the church in his makeshift diorama. "And where do you put it?"

"In the center of the town," Annie answered. "So it's easy for everyone to get to."

"Yes," Dr. Burns agreed. "Churches were the immigrant version of a Roman marketplace or a Greek agora. These weren't just houses of spirituality, but the places people went to meet with their neighbors each weekend. To socialize."

He grabbed the pepper shaker, placing it down the way.

"And after church, you might need to pick up essentials. Which would lead you to..."

"The corner store," Annie said.

"Very good," Dr. Burns nodded as if he were applauding a particularly clever student. "Remember, immigrants didn't have Target. There was no Walmart. They had to rely on local services run by sole proprietors. That's why Sophia Barnak's corner store is such a central tenant of my research. Her store allowed the community to flourish because they didn't have to journey miles away for supplies. A woman of that time running such a pivotal service to the community was remarkable. My argument— my thesis, if you will— is that modern towns would benefit from creating cultural centers that mirror the geography of historical settlements. The old can influence the new. How can we learn from the past to create connections in the future? Our modern cities and towns are isolated, spoiled for choice. How we can create a sense of belonging just through our placement of basic services? The corner store is an important piece in the puzzle I'm presenting."

"Was the family open to your research being conducted on their property?" Annie asked.

"It took some convincing," Dr. Burns said. "But they eventually came around."

Annie paused, the look in her eyes telling Ethan she wanted to pry more deeply, but had thought better of it. There were times Annie would push her subjects and times in which she would take a gentler hand. Knowing which strategy to use at a given time was one of Annie's greatest superpowers.

"What's your ultimate goal with this research?" Annie moved on.

"To renew my grant, I'm afraid," Dr. Burns said calmly. "We've passed our first landmark and are now competing to win the second. With each round of funding, the amount of money increases but so do the expectations. I have to convince the foundation that supplied the grant that our research has merit and is worth re-investing in. We're asking them to double down, essentially. I believe that Sunray is a perfect case study for the argument I'm making. This community proves that the design of a town influences health and well-being for generations to come. The fact that so many legacy residents still live here proves the thesis. It even gives us the chance to compare the happiness of modern-day residents to those from generations back using first-hand interviews, journal pages, and anecdotal accounts. There's much to mine, here."

"The family gave you a key to the corner store," Annie said, crossing her legs casually as if the question were no more important than any that came before. "Have you used it?"

"Only once," Dr. Burns flushed. "But to be honest, I misplaced it."

"When?" Annie asked.

"Weeks ago," Dr. Burns shrugged. "I'm not the neatest person, what with all the papers and research that end up spread around my hotel room. I thought I had it safely secured in my desk and now it's disappeared."

"Then how have you been accessing the store?"

"Paul's been letting me in," Dr. Burns responded. "He's quite the solid keeper of the property. He has a flexible schedule, considering him and his wife live close by. He's always been available when I call, and unlocks the place for me when I want to look around, or take some photographs for the final paper."

"Has he left you in the space alone?" Annie asked. A suspicion was tingling the edges of her arm and she couldn't resist but to chase it in case it might lead to a fact.

"Well, yes, I guess he did," Dr. Burns admitted. "But why would that matter?" Dr. Burns shook his head. "You understand I'm a researcher committed to preserving the mysteries of the past? Paul knew he could trust me with the space. No one cares more than I do about making sure the legacy of Sophia's corner store lives on."

"Of course," Annie agreed. "I can see that's true. I wish, for Paul's sake, someone would have cared about his life as much as *you* care about history." She smiled brightly and then stood, indicating the meeting was over. "Thank you so much for your time," she said, reaching out to shake Dr. Burns' hand. "We'll be in touch if we have any more questions."

Annie and Ethan left the small Bed & Breakfast, and Dr. Burns sat back down on the couch, extracting a notebook from his bag. He'd intended to stay in the lobby today, reading over his most recent observations and perhaps beginning to work on the abstract for his next publication. But now, as he tried to focus on the page in front of him, the sinking feeling in his stomach distracted him from the task.

Dr. Burns thought about the key that was hiding under the side table in his room and hoped that he'd made the right decision by claiming he'd lost it. In retrospect, losing the key was a dull excuse. He was a clever man. Why hadn't he thought of something better? Perhaps he should have owned up to having a key, but stated he never used it. Losing the key was too convenient. Too contrived.

Dr. Burns' stomach turned. He packed up his notebook at once, grabbing his bag and rushing to his rented room, suddenly feeling that he was about to be sick.

CHAPTER ELEVEN

VERONICA

VERONICA HAD WORN her best blazer for the meeting she was currently conducting at her modest office space. Even though the meeting was with two detectives investigating a murder case and not about Real Estate, Veronica still dressed for success. She'd been trained to see every new acquaintance as a potential lead. Who knew? Maybe the detectives sitting in front of her— Annie and Ethan— would want to buy property in Sunray, and someday come back to her as clients.

Veronica spun around in her desk chair, looking very small in her large, empty office. She sat behind the desk, smiling over it at her two guests.

"I'm so glad you're on top of things," Veronica said, teeth shining. "Sunray is not this kind of place. These sorts of things never happen here. I'd hate for people moving into the area to get the idea that it isn't safe. Our crime rate is incredibly low. And we have a great high school just down the road."

"Do many people move into the area?" Annie asked. "I got the impression most residents inherited the land as it was passed down to them."

"That's true," Veronica admitted. "Most of us who live in Sunray grew up here. Lifers is what they call us. I'm one of them," she said proudly. "My family owns a farm just down the road."

"You didn't want to go into the farming business?" Annie asked a surprised tone in her voice.

"Well, n-no…" Veronica stammered. "My family has done quite well for themselves, but the farm life wasn't for me. I always envisioned myself more like, I don't know," she paused thinking. "Have you seen *Sex and the City*?"

"Who hasn't?!" Annie exclaimed.

"Me," Ethan raised his hand, but everyone present ignored him.

"Well, I'm more of a Miranda than a Charlotte," Veronica offered. "I always wanted to have a career that involved financial transactions, or closing deals. Just something…"

"Fancy?" Annie said.

"Kind of," Veronica agreed. "It's not that farming isn't fun. I just don't really like animals. Or getting dirty. I wanted to wear cute heels and network and talk to people from all over the world..."

"I'm surprised you didn't move into the city," Annie said.

Veronica noticeably bristled. "Well, the complicated part is, I like Sunray. This is my home. I *want* to be here. I just also want to be *myself* here. Does that make any sense?"

"No—" Ethan started to say, but Annie elbowed him in the ribs before he could get the word out.

"Of course it does," Annie agreed. "What's your vision for Sunray, in terms of Real Estate?"

Veronica brightened, happily surprised to have found someone who saw where she was trying to go— the path she was hoping to tread. "It's so funny you asked!" Veronica said. She clicked on her keyboard, opening up a Pinterest board on her computer. She turned the monitor around to give Annie and Ethan a better view.

"There's so much potential here," she said, nodding at the collection of images. A digital vision board showed pictures

Veronica saved under the title "FUTURE SUNRAY." An image of a tall apartment complex, complete with a swimming pool and dog park sat in the corner of the page. It was followed by a community center with an advertisement for pilates classes in one of the towering glass windows. Next to it was a picture of a grand hotel, marble steps leading up to an enormous French-inspired facade. "I think Sunray could be the next urban center, over time of course. We have so much open land that could be developed. If the right businesses came in, we could see the whole place explode."

"That's ambitious," Annie said, startled at the scale of Veronica's vision.

"We could build something really special here if people would be open to selling to developers. But there's some resistance," Veronica shrugged, closing the Pinterest page. "Most of the sales keep the land designated for farming use only instead of coffee shops and pilates studios. But hey, a girl can dream."

"Just out of curiosity, if someone owned land in an area that was building up, that land might become worth more in value, correct?" Annie asked, pretending not to know the answer.

"It happens," Veronica agreed. "Imagine owning a vacant lot in Manhattan one hundred years ago. It'd be worth a fortune today," she sighed, a wistful looking flashing across her face.

"And that's your goal for Sunray?" Annie pressed. "To see it become an urban center?"

Veronica tucked her hair behind her ears, settling back into her chair as if it suddenly struck that she'd gotten carried away and overshared. Annie tended to have that effect on people.

"My only goal right now is to serve the community," Veronica said. "Whatever they need, I'm here. I'm in the process of chasing down leads and have amassed quite a client list. It seems everyone is excited to work with someone just starting out in their career. I'm hungry and that's the difference. I'm a real go-getter, and my clients appreciate that."

"I get that impression," Annie agreed. "When the family back West signed up with you, they must have been thrilled."

"They were definitely impressed with my pitch," Veronica glowed. "I explained to them over the phone that I'm a unique blend of old and new. I'm a legacy resident of Sunray and I understand what makes the area special because my family's lived here for generations. But I also have a fresh, young perspective about what could happen here. I'm not stuck in my ways like some other lifers. They really responded to that idea and they signed up with me on the spot."

"Do other residents of Sunray resist change?" Annie asked.

"Sometimes," Veronica shrugged. "The historical society can be a real drag. But as long as you steer clear of them, you're golden."

"And the owners gave you a key to the corner store?"

"To show potential buyers," Veronica nodded. "The corner store itself doesn't have as much value nowadays, to be honest. It's the land itself that's worth the money, and the store is a tear-down. But the family let the corner store stand because it means to much to the community. The key was kind of an afterthought because the store itself isn't a draw for a buyer."

"And Paul was running the store?" Annie asked.

"Yes," Veronica nodded. "He and his wife own the property behind the Barnak lot. He'd open the store up for a few hours each evening. They don't sell too much on a daily basis. Maybe some local produce, a couple of bags of trail mix, a soda here and there. But he kept his word to the family and made sure the place ran. He used to go there a lot as a kid. I think it meant something to him."

"So he worked his own farm during the day, and managed

the store at night?" Annie said, surprised. "That's long hours isn't it?"

"Paul was that kind of guy," Veronica said, a strange edge to her voice. "Sunray was everything to him."

"You two got along then?" Annie asked, once again following a suspicion that might lead to a fact.

"We didn't interact much," Veronica soured, unable to stop her lip from curling up in the corner. "Can't say I spent enough time with him to feel one way or another." She cleared her throat, glancing at her watch like she'd just remembered something. "If you don't mind, I have another client to get to. It's been so busy lately, with all these show-ings. I'm worried I've taken on more clients than I can handle, but that's the way for career women like us, am I right?" She reached out to shake Annie's hand, and then Ethan's. "If you know anyone who's looking to buy or sell, here's my card." She reached into her bag, extracting a thin business card. "I'm licensed all throughout Virginia, not just Sunray. Always interested in expanding."

"We'll pass it along," Ethan assured her. He headed for the exit, both he and Annie recognizing they had been dismissed. As they stepped out onto the sidewalk, Annie glanced at a coffee shop across the street.

"We should grab a cup of coffee," she said. "Wait her out. See if she leaves for her so-called 'clients.'"

"You don't think she has any?" Ethan asked. He'd been getting the same impression but had no evidence to support his feeling that Veronica was a phony.

"Did you see the wall behind her?" Annie answered. "All those hooks waiting for keys. All of them are empty. She's in trouble."

"In that case, I *could* use a cup of coffee," Ethan agreed, taking Annie's hand in his and leading her across the street, where he knew they'd wait for hours for a woman who had no reason to leave her office at all.

CHAPTER TWELVE
RIGGS

RIGGS WAS DRIVING the van with the ceiling panels wide open as he answered Annie's questions. He had rigged the van to serve every need he had. The need for food. The need for shelter. And most importantly, the need for adventure. To this end, Riggs had created a convertible top that folded in on itself, its metal defense becoming an open air experience, like that of a convertible sedan.

His accomplice— Seth— was behind the wheel, careening the van down a dirt road at a speed better suited for highways. Riggs stood in the back with his arms wide open, looking like a tour guide as he shouted over the wind, grabbing onto nearby seats for balance as the van sped over the bumpy road.

"We like to do high-speed scans of the surrounding area," Riggs shouted at Annie and Ethan, who were seated on a small couch that was built into the wall.

Riggs pointed upward at a fixture toward the front of the van. It was a sphere, its glass, ocular shape conjuring images of an eye. It was affixed to the exterior shell of the driver's area, and as the van sped along, it rotated left and right. Annie couldn't help but think of the GoogleMaps street cars she sometimes saw passing through various cities she visited, all of them photographing the roads for use in the Google Maps program.

"It's LIDAR technology," Riggs shouted, pointing at the sphere on the front of the van. "It's mapping this entire area, creating a scan we can input into the computer."

"And that's useful... why?" Ethan shouted back, clutching the edge of the small couch he sitting on.

"There's more treasure than what's underground my man," Riggs laughed. "Every place we go, we look for ways to earn our keep. These scans can be sold to private companies for thousands of dollars. Mapping software applications. Private buyers. Even geologists and climate change researchers. LIDAR doesn't just give you an image of the surface. It tells you what's underground."

"Your website says you define yourself as a treasure-hunter," Annie said, her hair blowing in the wind. "How exactly would you define that term?"

"A treasure hunter is someone who sees opportunity everywhere, and isn't afraid to dig a little to get the payoff," Riggs said. Riggs called over his shoulder to his partner behind the wheel, "Seth, how would you define it?"

"Living feral!" Seth shouted back.

"He's right," Riggs agreed. "You gotta be a person who likes the chase. If you're a treasure hunter, you got no home, no roots, no routine. You have to be the kind of person who can just pick up and leave when that's how it's gotta be."

"And how long have you two been—" Annie motioned between Seth and Riggs, "—partners in this?"

"Since college," Riggs said. "I was doing my post-doc running a lab. Seth was one of my indentured-servant under-grads, paying off his student loans by helping us at night. When I dropped out to go chase a big find, he practically begged to come with me."

"Don't believe that bullshit!" Seth shouted over his shoulder. "He cried when he thought I wasn't coming. Said he couldn't do without me. Total baby, this one."

The van hit a deep pothole and some books on the back wall went flying. Annie clutched Ethan's arm to stay upright as Seth pulled hard on the wheel, taking the van around a corner. There was a skidding noise as the back tires whipped around, but somehow—the van stayed upright.

"You've made some improvements to the vehicle?" Annie said, trying her best to smile.

"This baby is indestructible," Riggs offered. "These tires? They're what you'd put on a military vehicle. The roof is a custom add-on. So's the kitchen and the bathroom. It's our home away from home. Might have had a couple of other special features put in, just for fun. Isn't that right, Seth?"

"Copy!" Seth said, reaching for a button on the dashboard. There was an exploding sound from the rear of the vehicle. Annie and Ethan whirled around, their eyes looking up into the wide open sky. A firework burst up above them, red and blue sparks shooting into the air.

"That one was just for fun," Riggs said. "Or in case we need to get away from some unsavory types."

"Do you run into a lot of those on your travels?" Annie asked.

"Here's the thing about treasure hunting," Riggs said. "People get so desperate— so fixated on what they want— they lose themselves. I've seen guys mess with each other's air tanks on dives to look at sunken ships, all because they wanted to be the first to find a single gold coin. It's a dirty business."

"Why Sunray?" Annie continued her line of questioning. "There's got to be bigger money in antiquities, but you're here in a small Virginia town, looking for some buried treasure on a farm. Why?"

"Well," Riggs scratched his head. "I may or may not have a warrant out for my arrest in a few countries— big misunderstanding, but try to tell *them* that— and if I leave the US, there are places that would extradite me. If I stay home, I'm safe. The problem is, the good old US of A is a pretty new country by global standards, so we don't have too much of the ancient stuff. Colonial is about as close as it gets. And indigenous."

"I see," Annie nodded. "That must be frustrating."

"I'm enjoying it more than I thought I would," Riggs said. "There's some pluses to staying a little closer to what's familiar. When the family reached out to me about the corner store, they were thrilled I was available. When you take these smaller jobs, there's something more personal about it. Right, Seth?"

"Whatever you say, boss," Seth called back.

"Can you tell me more about this supposed treasure?" Annie asked. "I've heard from other locals that Sophia claimed she buried something on the land upon her death. But that was thirty years ago. Why does the family have reason to believe it wouldn't have been found by now?"

"Lady," Riggs leaned on the chair in front of him, looking at Annie. "Jewels worth millions of dollars lie on the ocean floor for hundreds of years. I've seen ancient Egyptian canopic jars worth hundreds of thousands shoved in a box in an old man's attic while his family panhandles to survive. Valuable things get overlooked every day. People don't know what they have. And if they don't have it, they don't know where to look. That's where I step in to help 'em."

"So why the renewed interest from the family?"

"They said they got a letter when they put the house up for sale. Someone claiming they knew Sophia back in the day and she told them the treasure was real. They claimed she told 'em she had *płynne złoto*, liquid gold."

"What makes the family so sure Sophia even had a treasure? If she'd had it, what could it have been?"

Riggs laughed as the van hit another pothole, making his way over a bookshelf on the back wall. He pulled out a thick binder filled with hole-punched research papers. The van lurched as he laid the binder spread eagle on the table, flipping to the appropriate tab.

"This here is Sophia's Ellis Island signature. Her maiden name was Wachowski. She married Frank Barnak upon arrival in Sunray, and became a Barnak." He flipped to the next page. "But the Wachowski's had a family history connecting them to the *Szlachta*— the Polish Royalty before the monarchy fell in the early 1900s. They were Royal, but didn't make a fuss about it. You know, once being royal wasn't so popular after the revolution."

"I wouldn't either," Ethan agreed. "Sounds like a great way to lose your head."

"Exactly," Riggs agreed. "But the Wachowski's were rumored to have managed to keep some of the *Szlachta's* royal jewels when the family ruled no more. Including— this one—"

He flipped to another page, revealing a painting of a stunning pendant necklace. A chain of pearls cascaded down to an enormous, oval-cut canary diamond. It was dark yellow in shade— so dark as to almost seem amber. In the painting, it sat on a woman's neck, enormously heavy and ostentatious.

"Notice the color?" Riggs asked. "That's the *zloto* diamond, or rather, *The Golden Diamond*. So-named for its golden hue. It was owned by the Polish aristocracy and disappeared after the monarchy fell. But Sophia was a close enough relative... what better way to hide the diamond than to pass it off to your niece, who was headed for America? And we believe Sophia's reference to liquid gold may have been connected to the diamond."

"Seems like a stretch," Ethan said, shaking his head. "It's all circumstantial evidence. You're putting in a lot of time and effort based on speculation."

"Hey," Riggs shrugged. "Sometimes you've gotta follow a hunch. I'm sure this one understands," he nodded at Annie, who didn't indicate her agreement, but instead, chewed on the inside of her cheek.

"Suspicions can *lead* to facts," Annie agreed. "But a person should act on facts alone."

"That's what we're here diggin' up," Riggs said, defensive. "Facts. Besides, if the gem turns out to be a cold lead, we'll be fine. There's other interests here."

"What other interests?" Annie asked.

"Sophia said she hid some kind of treasure on the property," Riggs shrugged. "Even if it isn't what we hoped for... if it's there, we'll find it."

The van lurched around another corner, and everyone held on tight as the centripetal force pushed the group into far windows.

"Almost there," Riggs nodded at the skyline. "Circle's about done and we'll break for lunch, roger that, Seth?"

"A beer and a stack of ribs!" Seth shouted back in agreement.

"I'll make this brief then," Annie said, eager to exit the van and escape the wild ride she was on. "You had a key to the corner store, is that correct?"

"A key to the corner store and access to the entire property," Riggs agreed. "See, the family out West trusts me. When they found me on the internet, they practically begged me to come out here. They knew I was one of only a handful of people equipped to get to the bottom of a missing treasure, and out of the handful, I'm the best."

"So you're able to enter and exit the corner store at any time of day or night?"

"Yes," Riggs agreed.

"What interactions, if any, did you have with Paul Kaminski?" Annie asked.

"He was fine," Riggs shrugged. "A little surly sometimes but seemed committed to the job. I don't think he liked us bein' there, but he didn't have much say in the matter."

"Were you familiar with his routine? How did he spend an average day?"

"Well, he had his own farm to manage," Riggs rubbed a thoughtful hand on his chin. "But his wife took care of most of that. The rest of the time he was either at the bar or opening up the store. He made sure it was open at the hours the neighborhood needed most, but closed it right up to get home at night."

"Did ever tell you anything about the treasure?" Annie hedged. "If there were something buried you'd think he would have found it."

"Never said a word," Riggs said. Then, he paused as if something had just hit him. A syrupy look in his eye gave Annie the distinct impression he was angling to change the subject. "Actually," Riggs said, a light in his eyes. "There was something. A day before the murder, he told me he knew that the sale wasn't going to go through."

"The sale of the property?" Annie asked.

"Yes," Riggs nodded. "I ran into him while running some metal detectors over the topsoil— just looking for loose ends before we go deeper— and he said I didn't need to rush anymore because the sale was about to be called off."

"How did he know that for certain?"

"No idea," Riggs shrugged. "But he mentioned it like it was a fact, and one day later— he was dead."

There was a screeching sound as Seth slammed on the brakes and the van lurched to a halt.

"Time for my ribs!" Seth shouted over his shoulder. Outside the windows sat a barbecue restaurant, smoke rising from behind the building. The savory scent of salted meat clung to the air, a bold invitation.

"You all care to join us?" Riggs asked. Annie shook her head.

"I think we'll take ours to go," she said, glancing at their rental car, which was still parked in front of the restaurant.

The group had met here to carpool in the van, and they'd made a complete circle around Sunray in the past hour. "Thank you for your time," Annie said, shaking Riggs' hand.

Ethan did the same and then passed him a business card. "If you think of anything else, you can reach us at this number."

Riggs nodded, watching as the pair jumped down the van steps and headed for their rental car. He thought he'd done a good job pointing them toward a trail that led away from him. That was the thing about being a treasure hunter— you had to know which leads to follow, and which leads to drop. With any luck, he'd set them on a path that would protect his interests.

"Call again anytime you need!" Riggs shouted after them, hoping very much they would never, *ever* call again.

CHAPTER THIRTEEN

KAREN

"COME ON IN, don't mind the mess," Karen Kaminski said as she ushered Annie and Ethan into her home. They'd been standing on the wrap-around front porch— the summer heat making beads of sweat cling to their skin— but as they entered the front door, a wave of cool air offered relief.

"Are you remodeling?" Ethan asked, staring at the mess in front of him. Plastic sheets hung over the walls of the quaint home, and buckets of paint sat on the foyer floor. Overhead, disconnected wires hung from the ceiling, and an antique light fixture lay beneath it, apparently discarded. On a bare piece of wooden shiplap paneling, three different paint colors had been wiped onto the wall in order to compare the effect. A pastel, spring green. A bright, summer yellow. And a bold, cobalt blue.

"Not remodeling exactly, but just trying out something new," Karen said, unable to keep the excitement out of her voice. "I thought I could use some changes around here given —" she paused, trying not to address her husband's murder directly "— everything that's happened." She motioned down the hallway, urging Annie and Ethan forward. "We'll sit in the kitchen," she said, encouraging. "It's the only room that's not a disaster right now. We can leave the screen door open and look out at the cows."

Annie and Ethan followed her, arriving at an immaculate kitchen with original cabinets and linoleum flooring. Karen moved to the side door and swung it open, leaving the screen behind it closed so the warm air circulated into the space. "Nice to get some fresh air," Karen said, looking out the screen at the horizon in the distance. "That's Betty over there," she pointed at an enormous female cow who was grazing on a wide patch of land. "She likes to eat on the west side, don't ask me why."

"Wasn't 'gonna," Ethan said. He took a seat at the table next to Annie, who was already lost in thought, glancing around the room as she considered what evidence might surround her.

"You have a lovely home," Annie said, watching as Karen dipped into the refrigerator and pulled out a pitcher of tea, which she promptly poured into three glasses. "We appreciate you having us here during such a difficult time."

Karen sat down at the table, and for a moment looked as if she had no idea what Annie was talking about. Then, the words clicked. *A difficult time.* Suddenly, Karen's eyes dropped to the floor, and her face shifted, giving the impression of a grieving widow. "Yes," Karen said, trying her best to nod. "It is, isn't it? But of course you're welcome. Anything you can do to get to the bottom of this is appreciated. I want to know who killed my husband. Any wife would want to know."

"Of course," Annie agreed. "You have our word we'll do everything we can to get answers." Annie looked out the screen door at Betty the cow, who was chewing in a calm, circular pattern. "Are you concerned about running the farm alone?" Annie asked. "It must take a lot of work, considering how much land you have."

"I've been running the farm alone for years," Karen waved

a hand in the air as if she wasn't concerned. "Paul had other interests. He was responsible for what we call the side businesses. Selling fresh milk from Betty at the market. Managing Sophia's corner store. We have bees in the back and our own line of local jarred honey. Paul handled all of that, and me? I handled the farm. The crop rotation. The animals. The day-to-day running. It's hard work but at this point I've got it on autopilot. The key is," she leaned in, a glint in her eyes. "You get up early while it isn't too hot. Around 5 am. And you knock out all the things that need doing. But noon, I'm a free woman." She leaned back in her chair. "It's a beautiful life, being connected to the land you live on."

"You seem to love it," Annie agreed. "But it must have been hard, not seeing Paul very much. It sounds like the two of you were ships in the night."

"He was my husband," Karen bristled, looking offended but trying to hide it. "I'm upset he 's gone."

"Of course you are!" Annie agreed. "I just meant it must have been hard having different schedules."

"It was," Karen said, and she left it at that.

"Paul of course had a key to the corner store," Annie said, sensing it was time to move on to other questions. "Did he have any enemies? Anyone who might have had it out for him?"

"If he did, he never told me about 'em," Karen said. She stared at the ceiling, considering possibilities. "Was anything taken from the store?" Karen asked. "Could it have been a robbery and Paul got it the way? It would be like him, to pick a fight over the place. He was more concerned with the store than our own house. Obsessed with it, you might say."

"Nothing was taken," Annie said. "So I don't suspect a robbery. There was no sign of forced entry. The crime felt more— personal. Either Paul let this individual into the store after hours, or the person who killed him had a key and knew he would be there."

"My goodness, I told the family out West they should stop giving out keys like candy," Karen shook her head. "It was better when just Paul, Gladys, and I had access. The three of us own lots right next to each other." She pointed out the window at a brown fence designating the property line. "Don't know if you talked to Gladys yet—"

"We did," Annie confirmed.

"— well she says we're the original three," Karen continued. "Her house. Paul and me. And Sophia's land. We're what's left of the original Sunray. Sure, there are other lots scattered about, but ours are connected and always have been. There's something special about that, if you ask Paul or Gladys."

"But not you?" Annie pressed.

Karen shrugged. "This land belonged to Paul and his family. He was a man who clung to things from the past. I'm an artist and always considering what could be in the future. But we made living' here work because he got his family heritage, and I got my time to think. Farms are good places for dreamin'."

"Ethan's a city boy. He's not big on being so far away from a Cheesecake Factory."

"We've got one twenty minutes down the road," Karen told him.

"Still too far," Ethan answered. "I like to be able to walk to get my cheesecake."

"Those are beautiful mugs, by the way," Annie pointed at a serving tray positioned near the sink, a growing display of three mugs sitting on top. Each mug exhibited a different pattern. The first had a patchwork, hand-painted design. The second featured scalloped roses. And the third was solid clay, particularly remarkable in that it featured no handle. Faded animals ran across its surface— running antelope and buffalo making Annie think of ancient cave paintings. It looked to be quite old. If it was a replica of something ancient— it was a convincing one.

"Thank you," Karen beamed. "They're beautiful aren't they?"

"They are," Annie said. "How many do you have?"

"Just a few," Karen shrugged. "It's a growing collection. A friend gave me the idea. Said nothing in life should be exactly the same. So I decided to mix up the dining ware."

"That one in particular is quite special," Annie said, nodding at the mug with faded animals running across the surface. "I like it so much I may ask you if I can pour my tea in it?"

Annie stared at her, deadpan and serious in the request. Karen blinked, a horrified expression crossing her face.

"Oh, that one's not to be used," she said lightly. "It's special. It's just for display. It's quite old actually."

"So I *can't* pour my tea in it?" Annie confirmed. Karen looked at her as if she'd lost her mind.

"No," Karen shrugged, her countenance displaying the mildest shade of anger. "As I said before, you *can't*. It's an artifact, not for use."

"I see. And you're mixing up the house itself, what with all the remodeling," Annie added, smiling at her. "How long have you been renovating?"

"How long?" Karen's voice caught in her throat. "Oh, I don't know—"

"It's just..." Annie said, her tone casual. "That paint on the wall looked new. The samples are still wet."

"Well, I've been trying to decide on the color for a while," Karen answered.

"*You've* been trying to decide, or you and Paul?"

Karen didn't answer.

"Excuse me for being so rude," Annie said genuinely, "but I just know how hard it must be to renovate without him."

"Difficult, yes," Karen said.

There was a long silence as Annie took Karen in, studying her every movement.

"Were you happy with Paul?" she asked.

Karen snorted. "Of course— who *isn't* happy they're married? You get married," she rambled, unsure of exactly what she was trying to say. "You do it. Because— that's what people do. You get married. And you're happy. Or you're not. But you're married. And that's that."

"I see," Annie said. She leaned in. "Is there anything else we should know about Paul?"

"Nothing," Karen answered, looking out the screen door in the distance. She changed the subject with ease. "Betty looks hot. Might need to get her some ice." She kept her gaze fixed on Betty, her glazed expression saying she'd gone somewhere else— somewhere Annie and Ethan couldn't reach her.

"They ice the cows?" Ethan whispered to Annie, who didn't respond.

"We'll leave you to it," Annie said to Karen, pulling Ethan out of his seat. "We can show ourselves out. Thank you again, for having us. And those mugs— they really are beautiful. That one in particular."

With that, Annie and Ethan left. When she heard the front door slam, Karen stood and wandered toward the window, still looking out at Betty.

She knew she should have waited to start repainting. But Paul had always wanted things so *sterile*. Karen couldn't help herself. The moment she had an opportunity to make her life more colorful, she'd taken it without hesitation.

And now, it was about to be her undoing.

CHAPTER FOURTEEN

LATER, Annie and Ethan sat together at a Cheesecake Factory, located in the nearby community of Norfolk, just a short drive East of Sunray. Annie stared down at her cheeseburger, hating that she was still delighted at a familiar favorite.

"You were serious about the Cheesecake Factory," Annie said to Ethan, the hanging lights overhead casting a soothing, golden shadow over their meal.

"You were the one who brought it up," Ethan answered, taking a bite of his own burger. "Worth the drive. This actually isn't so bad. Being away from everything, I mean. Makes you appreciate a good thing more once you get it."

"So farm life could be for you?" Annie asked, a distant look in her eyes.

"Not yet," Ethan said, mouth full. "Sorry to disappoint. Although I'll admit, when I think about the Real Estate ripper — that he might be someone in uniform— moving sounds pretty good."

Annie let her elbows rest on the table, sensing a deeper question in Ethan's voice. "We can't run from what happened. Even if we moved tomorrow to someplace totally off the grid, it wouldn't matter. Because the case would still live in our heads."

"I know," Ethan said, glancing down at his plate. "But it's just this idea that there's us, and there's them. The Real Estate Ripper could be one of *us*. Someone in uniform, or who's supposed to be fighting for the truth. It bothers me that we don't know who we can trust."

"We do know who we can trust," Annie reached a hand across the table and put it over Ethan's. "We've got *us* right here."

Ethan nodded, but Annie could tell that the idea of the Real Estate Ripper being a person in uniform still bothered him. He'd always placed his faith in organizations that fought for truth and justice. He liked the simplicity of the idea there were good guys and bad guys. But recently, Ethan had come to realize there could be both on either side. And Annie— whose mind was so practiced at assembling pieces in a meaningful order— could see that he had yet to make sense of it. "If we can't trust the FBI or the Police, we'll find new people to trust," Annie offered. "Simple as that. One way or another, we'll find what we need."

Ethan nodded, finishing off the last of his burger.

"Should we debrief?" Ethan asked, hopeful that moving Annie toward another subject would distract her from the more complicated questions brewing beneath the surface.

"Let's start with Karen and work backward," Annie agreed. "She's moving on rather quickly, isn't she?"

"I thought the same," Ethan said. "There's no love loss there. If I get shot on the job one day, please mourn me for at least six months."

"You?" Annie laughed. "I'd be inconsolable for a year, minimum Then I'd find a new boyfriend with great abs. But he *still* wouldn't have your sense of humor. That's one of a kind."

"Appreciate it," Ethan said with a mock bow. "So you think Karen's behavior crosses the line of what's normal?"

"Normal is different for everyone," Annie thought out loud. "But I can't say she wasted any time on the home renovation. Paul's been gone two days and she's already picking new paint colors. But that's a suspicion, not a fact. What's a *fact* is that she failed to mention a police report filed regarding a domestic dispute between the two of them."

"I don't remember that from her file," Ethan said.

"It was compliments of Milo," Annie said. "She may have retracted the filing, but he found in the Police archives. Used something called a digital time machine."

"So there was a domestic dispute between the two of them? That would explain the lack of mourning. That doesn't mean she killed him, though."

"It doesn't," Annie weighed the idea. "But the fact she fails to mention it is certainly incriminating." She took a sip of her drink, allowing images of the potential suspects to flip through her mind's eye. "Next we have Riggs, the treasure hunter."

"Is he for real?" Ethan asked. "It's like he thinks he's Indiana Jones or something. The way they drive that van around— it's a public hazard is what it is."

Annie smiled to herself, getting the idea Ethan felt a certain insecurity around Riggs, who seemed to trigger something deep within him. Maybe it was the reckless abandon with which Riggs lived his life— it was a trait some women might find appealing.

"Totally irresponsible," Annie agreed. "I like guys who drive with safety in mind."

"So Mad Max over there is in town to find a gem. Doesn't seem like a motivation for murder."

"No, but his file showed he's in financial trouble," Annie said. "I want to talk to the family out West about him. Get their thoughts."

"We'll set up a call," Ethan agreed. "What's your take on Veronica?"

"She's ambitious," Annie tapped her fingers on the table, remembering the look in Veronica's eyes when she showed them her vision board for Sunray's much more urban future. "She's also unrealistic. Young. Has no idea what she's doing. I sense desperation in her. But it's not her so much as the sale. I need to understand who was interested in buying the property and why."

"Another question for the family," Ethan agreed. "That brings us to Dr. Burns..."

"The star researcher," Annie nodded. "His file paints quite a different picture. He's a lackluster member of the faculty, with very few recent publications. The grant money he brings in is minuscule at best. There's something more, there, that he isn't sharing."

"That leaves our final contestant," Ethan tapped his hands on the table in a fake drumroll, "Gladys. Any ideas?"

"It's against her personality profile not to call the phone tree in such a dramatic event," Annie said. "I find that odd, to say the least. She mentioned the brother and sister who were renting the land before the family put it up for sale— I'd like to speak to them at some point. See what they think about Gladys, considering they lived next to her." Annie paused, her eyes glazing over as if lost in a daydream. "I keep picturing Gladys sitting on her porch, watching all this happening," Annie said, the image bright and perfect in her mind. "Sitting in that rocking chair, doing absolutely nothing while she has the juiciest news to report to the phone tree. It's so inconsistent with her personality profile and who I believe her to be. There's more to her than meets the eye." Annie paused. "I wonder what she's doing right now?"

CHAPTER FIFTEEN
GLADYS

THE MUD STUCK TO GLADYS' boots as she marched toward the tractor. The dark, evening air clung to her skin, the sound of crickets chirping in the distance a comforting companion and a reminder that— at this time of night— the only witnesses to her crime would be ones that couldn't speak.

Gladys stomped her way to the tractor that was parked behind her house, resting at the Northern edge of her property line. She stepped up into the seat and revved the engine, listening to the soft purring sound that emanated from within. Gladys loved that sound. It was a noise that reminded her she could do anything, and that no challenge was too large in her wake.

The tractor's massive tires began to move as Gladys pushed on the accelerator, urging the vehicle forward as pieces of caked-on mud dropped from the bottom of her Hudson brand wellie boots. Gladys careened toward the edge of her property, braked for a moment to ensure no one was watching, and then drove the tractor straight forward onto Sophia Barnak's farm.

She surged towards the corner store, and for a moment it

looked as if she might drive straight into the ancient wooden structure and take the whole thing down. But just before impact, she moved the tractor to the left, rolling toward the back of the farm where tall trees marked the edge of the Dismal Swamp. Her tires sped over neat rows of seeds that would one day become a crop of soybeans, but Gladys didn't care if she interrupted their slumber: she was a woman on a mission.

Finally, Gladys arrived at her destination. It was a small plot of land on her neighbor's farm, marked by the tiniest of wooden fences. The border fence consisted of wooden stakes only one foot high, their arrangement subtly marking an area at the back of the farm that measured about fifteen feet by one hundred feet. Plants emerged from the soil— unlike the sleeping soybean seeds that were buried on the majority of the farm, this particular crop was already growing. Leaves emerged from the dirt, reaching toward the sky with a ferocious, green attack. The fronds looked like palm fans, their multiple leaves spreading wide around a single stem in groups of three.

Gladys looked at the plants with a deep longing. It was hard to let them go, but she knew what she had to do.

She revved the engine on the tractor, scooping up the dirt in front of her, and all the plants with it. She drove her first load toward the swamp through a hole in the trees, then dumped the dirt and plants into the water, where it promptly sunk to the bottom of the murky swamp as if it had never existed at all. Then, she headed back for another scoop.

Gladys repeated the process again and again, watching as the farm-within-a-farm became nothing but empty soil. It took dozens of trips back and forth between the swamp and the farm, but when Gladys was done, there wasn't a single sign of the plants she'd removed from her neighbor's property.

When the job was done, Gladys wiped a hand over her

brow, still seated on top of the tractor. She didn't think anyone had heard her until she noticed a light come on at the only other adjacent property besides her own:

Karen Kaminski's house. Paul's wife was awake.

Gladys shook her head. Karen wouldn't be a problem. That was another thing she loved about Sunray. Everybody knew each other.

Gladys turned the tractor back on without a hint of fear, forging a straight line that headed from Sophia Barnak's property back onto her own. When the tractor was settled safely back in its parking spot, Gladys jumped down and headed for the barn, grabbing two shovels— one in each hand.

She strode across the darkness, closing the distance between her own property and Karen's, where the light was still on in the kitchen window. When she reached the wraparound porch, she didn't bother to knock. Instead, Gladys shouted at the door.

"Karen? Honey?"

There was a moment, and then the door opened up. Karen crossed her arms, wearing nothing but a robe and pajamas.

"You up to no good again, Gladys?" Karen asked, arching her eyebrows in an amused, bothered way.

"What I else would I be doin' if I weren't up to no good?" Gladys snorted, holding out a shovel. "I demolished my solo enterprise."

"No," Karen's face fell. "That's a shame."

"Sure is," Gladys agreed. "It seems everyone has it out for women in business."

"That *is* a shame, although I believe I cautioned you not to engage in said enterprise— which I will claim until the day I die to know absolutely nothing about— when you first set out to do it, for multiple reasons—"

"—none of which we should rehash right now," Gladys interrupted. She held out a shovel, offering it to Karen. "I gotta cover the trail the tractor left in the mud."

"You can't be serious," Karen said, unable to believe Gladys would ask such a thing of her.

"'Course I am," Gladys answered. "The tracks lead straight to my house. You'd have to be an idiot to leave them there."

"Of all the things you've asked me to do over the years—"

"Isn't it more important what we ask each other *not* to do?" Gladys offered, a flint sparking in her eye. "And what we ask each other *not* to say? I'm real good at not talkin' for someone who loves the phone tree. Might say I've done you a solid by keeping secrets to myself. Can't you help a friend out?"

Karen considered, biting the edge of her lip.

"Crazy old coot," Karen finally said, taking the shovel from Gladys with a begrudging flip of her hair. Together, they walked back to their neighbor's farm, the two of them working backward to cover not just the tire tracks, but their own footprints in the mud. Their shovels swung in unison, and when they were done, they stood on Gladys' farm, looking out over the fresh soil. There wasn't a single sign that anything had happened at all.

Gladys punched Karen on the shoulder. "I appreciate you lending a hand, neighbor. You wanna come in for a snack? I just finished a batch of brownies."

"I'll bring some milk over," Karen agreed, yawning. "Betty's been offering the best lately."

CHAPTER SIXTEEN
DR. BURNS

DR. BURNS DRUMMED his fingers on the desk in his modest hotel room, staring at the landline telephone that sat in front of him. He was waiting for an important call and had been assured that the person in question would reach out to him today at 3 pm, on the dot. He glanced at the alarm clock on the bedside table:

It was now 3:15 pm.

Dr. Burns had never expected to be exceptional— instead, he had only hoped to be average. In fact, when he'd earned his PhD, it was due to a lengthy list of assistance he received in the form of family money, private tutors, mental health counseling, and nepotistic favoritism from his Uncle, who was the head of his department. Without any one of these things, Dr. Burns would never have been able to graduate given his struggles in academia. He recognized his privilege and knew he was lucky to have come from a position in the world that afforded him opportunities other people didn't have.

That was what made Dr. Burns' life so painful— he *knew*, without a doubt, that he was average. He had never been good in school. He had no athletic ability. No talent for music, or art. All he had ever wanted was to find a position where he could "middle." A job where he could continue being average without the threat of being fired. His parents— who were alarmingly exceptional themselves, with his mother being an astrophysicist and his father being an engineer— had wisely pushed him to become a professor. They encouraged him to seek a job with tenure so that— after passing the most rigorous and difficult tests up front— he would become close to unfireable. He chose to become a Professor of History because he found the study of the average person interesting. He was never impressed by the lives of Kings and Queens or famous leaders of thought— Dr. Burns had just wanted to know how the average person in a given time-period lived, and whether they'd been very happy or not.

Up until now, Dr. Burns had found his reasonable expectations met. It was difficult to land the academic job, but his Uncle had made some calls, and now— fifteen years later— he was fully unfireable and happy with where he'd landed.

Except for the matter of compensation.

Dr. Burns had watched the world around him change in the years since he'd been hired. Now, Universities rewarded flashy new hires with impressive research resumes and niche specialties of interest. Dr. Burns was surrounded by superstars, and his salary had failed to increase as a result. Dr. Burns had lied when he'd told the detectives he was well-compensated. The University expected their employees to compensate with grant funding to support their research, which was not Dr. Burns' strong suit.

And getting grant funding— meant being exceptional. Suddenly, the phone rang. Dr. Burns picked it up immediately.

"Hello?" he said, even though he knew exactly who it was. "No, that's fine, I was just working on a publication..."

He glanced down at the notepad in front of him, which

contained nothing but a couple of doodled illustrations of a house, a dog, and a palm tree. "Yes, I'm so happy we're taking this time to discuss—"

He paused as the voice on the other end muttered something, and his face fell. "I was hoping you'd say otherwise."

Dr. Burns looked out the window, his eyes foggy and distant. "See, the thing is," he said into the phone. "I'm already here. I'm continuing the research." The voice on the other end offered a startled retort. "I decided to continue anyway, even if the funding wasn't secured."

There was a question from the other end of the line.

"Why would I do a thing like that?" Dr. Burns repeated the question out loud. He felt something stir deep within him. It was a strange sort of rage that had been simmering there since he was a child. An indignation that lived deep in his belly, growing stronger with every year that passed. "I did it because *I* may not be exceptional, but *this place* is. I did it because there's history here that warrants documenting, and even if I'm not the best researcher the University has to offer, I'm the one who cares the most. And I did it because—"

He paused, trying to think of something meaningful to say.

"— because I *wanted* to." It sounded infantile, but what was done was done.

The voice on the other line muttered in protest.

"How am I paying for the hotel?" Dr. Burns repeated. "With my own money. It may shock you to learn this considering what you pay me at University, but I do happen to have some of my own." More mutters echoed from the line. "Yes, the expense reports are correct. I have *a lot* of money of my own and I'll spend it how I please. Are there any other questions about my private research, which I will publish *with or without* the University's support?"

There was no answer offered. Dr. Burns chose to accept the silence as a "no."

"Thank you for your time," Dr. Burns said, not meaning it at all. He slammed the phone down, a satisfying metallic sound bringing him crashing back to earth. He leaned back in his chair, horrified and surprised at himself.

What had he just done?

CHAPTER SEVENTEEN

RIGGS

"ARE you sure we should be in here so late?" Seth asked over Riggs' shoulder. They were inside Sophia Barnak's corner store, which looked worse for the wear. Police tape designated certain areas as banned from entry, and the items that had been knocked off shelves during the dispute still littered the floor. The only thing that remained untouched was a glowing *Coca-Cola* sign that had hung over the jukebox for decades. It was still plugged in, its neon light casting colors across the room.

"It's a crime scene now. Doesn't that change what we're allowed to do?"

"I didn't hear nobody say a thing to me about treating this place any different now that's a crime scene, did you?" Riggs answered. He stopped to examine a pile of trail mix that had been spilt across the bar.

"No..."

"Then I'm not changing what I'm here to do. The goal stays the same. Look for *liquid gold.* Any clues about the diamond. Now that Paul's outta the way we can really dig deep."

"I still don't get what the diamond has to do with the

store," Seth shrugged, taking a seat at a barstool as if he expected an invisible bartender to serve him up a drink. "If Sophia had the diamond, she would have buried it."

Riggs sighed. Seth was dull and inexperienced. He'd hired him for his loyalty and work ethic— not for his brains.

"The LiDAR scans don't show a thing buried under that dirt," Riggs said, pausing to look out the window at the vast acres of land outside. "If it were there, our scans would've found it. We've scanned half the town at this point—"

"I thought that was for Veronica—" Seth started to say stupidly, but Riggs cut him off.

"For the *tenth time...* we don't talk about that out *loud!*"

"Sorry," Seth shrugged.

"So if the diamond isn't underground," Riggs continued. "Maybe Sophia stored it in the corner store somewhere, all those years ago. The building is original. Maybe it just hasn't been found. When she said she buried something valuable on the property, maybe she meant in the walls, or under the floorboards."

Riggs paused, taking in the space, considering all the places Sophia Barnak could have hidden a precious item like *The Golden Diamond.* The floorboards. The rafters. Under the bar. The idea of the diamond being hidden in the store had occurred to Riggs before, but Paul had been resistant to allowing him to search the space thoroughly. Now that Paul was out of the way, Riggs saw before him a brief, shining opportunity to search the right way.

"We start with the floors," Riggs said. "I want every floor board pried up." He reached into his bag, extracting a crowbar and a pair of leather gloves, which he tossed to Seth. "You don't leave a single piece of wood untouched, understand?"

"What about you?" Seth asked.

"I'm starting with the walls," Riggs answered, pulling out a stethescope and a hammer. "Listening for blank spaces.

Seeing if there's a hole somewhere that hasn't been noticed. After that, we go to the rafters." He nodded at the seiling overhead, which still featured the store's original wood beams. "There could be an attic crawl space. And remember: a diamond won't just be sitting naked in the breeze. She'll have wrapped it in something. Either a piecce of cloth, or maybe even a box. Be open to the idea what you're looking at might not be exactly what it seems. Anything you find, you bring it to me."

"Got it," Seth said.

Now that a plan had been made, the two men began the painstaking process of ripping the place apart. One by one, Seth pried up the floorboards, examining the dusty crawl space underneath. Meanwhile, Riggs went to town on the walls, knocking on the boards one plank at a time. Original wallpaper coated every surface in soft shades of floral yell-low, projecting an image of trees on a hillside over the washed-out butter shade. The wallpaper's texture made it difficult to tell where one plank ended and another began. Every now and then, Riggs would find a plank that sounded like a hollow space existed behind it, and would pull back his hammer, breaking into the wall so he could check what lay behind. Each time, his search came up empty. After making sure the walls were empty, Riggs stood on a ladder that had been discarded in the storeroom and made his way to the small attic space, which was filled with old shipments and storage boxes. He threw them to the ground without care, seeking one thing and one thing only: a hiding spot for a diamond.

Hours later, and the corner store was a shadow of its former self. The floor boards lay pried up in a pile. Holes in the walls destroyed the seamless flow of the charming printed wallpaper. Discarded storage boxes littered the room.

"Kind of shame to have destroyed it, isn't it?" Seth asked, a sudden pang of regret making him pause.

"All finds come at a cost, kid," Riggs answered. "You'll learn that later."

"I know, it's just..." Seth thought aloud. "It's a piece of history, isn't it? This building hasn't changed much in over a hundred years. It's even got the original wallpaper..."

Riggs' mouth dropped open as he considered what his apprentace had just stumbled upon. "Say that again," Riggs ordered.

"The building hasn't changed much."

"No, the other part."

Seth thought for a moment, remembering his words. "I said... it's even got the original wallpaper."

Riggs stood, moving toward the back of the store. "The picture on the wallpaper is of a mountain with trees. Sophie said she buried whatever she hid. And I saw something when I was checking the walls. Didn't think much of it, but now..."

Riggs paused at a stretch of yellow wallpaper on the Eastern wall. Where the rest of the store's wallpaper was smooth and unblemished, this piece was wrinkled and ripped in some places, almost as if someone had pulled it back and then attempted to reseal it in the spot where the pattern of trees ended.

"If you take it off, it's not like you can just order more," Riggs said aloud. "This pattern probably doesn't exist anymore."

"What're you gettin' at?" Seth asked.

"She hid it," Riggs whispered. "She hid directions to the diamond behind the wallpaper." He noticed a corner of the paper that lifted off the wall, inviting him to take action. Riggs pulled, and the entire sheet came down. "There's nothin' here because someone already got to this one. But maybe the others..." He turned to Seth, pointing at the opposite wall. "Take down every sheet and check the back, make sure there's no paperwork stuck to it."

Seth nodded, and together they pulled the paper off the

walls, revealing hundreds of old, brown documents underneath. Deeds of sale. Insurance papers. Birth certificates. All of it tumbled out from behind the paper, as if it had just been waiting for the chance to be found.

"Save everything!" Riggs shouted at Seth. "Don't let a single piece get damaged."

When it was done, the wallpaper lay ripped and discarded in the middle of the room, having served its purpose in hiding what was most important. Riggs and Seth collected the documents and spread them out across the bar, trying to make sense of what they had found.

"Is this what I think it is?" Seth said, holding up a document and showing it to Riggs.

"Why, yes it is," Riggs smiled, glancing at the *Coca-Cola* sign on the far wall. "It's exactly what Sophia promised... *liquid gold.*"

"But that other sheet of wallpaper was already torn," Seth said, concerned. "Did somebody else get to the diamond first?"

"I don't know what they got," Seth answered, shoving aside the documents that were of less use to him and making a pile of only the relevant papers. "But these..." He smoothed out a stack of documents in particular, smiling down at them. "These right here *are* the diamond. We had it all wrong kid. Sophia though, she was always telling the truth. She really *did* own liquid gold. And we just found it. It wasn't a diamond at all. It was *this.*"

He patted Seth on the back, and Riggs couldn't help but feel his life had just changed forever. He had one more piece of important business to attend to tomorrow. And after that, he could claim his biggest treasure yet.

CHAPTER EIGHTEEN

MILO'S BOMB shelter of an apartment was starting to feel cozier, now that Ethan and Annie had warmed up to it.

"It's too many beans," Ethan said, examining a can he'd picked up from the stack of food supplies. "You need to add some canned fruit. Otherwise, you could get scurvy."

"It's all about a protein-heavy diet my man," Milo said, spinning around in his office chair. He was seated in front of the bank of monitors, projecting information about their potential suspects up on the screens. "I've got scurvy covered in the vitamin section."

"Where's that?" Ethan asked.

Milo pointed at a fake statue of a bear that sat on a nearby shelf. "Squeeze his nose," Milo ordered.

Ethan looked at Annie, holding out a hand as if giving her the honors.

"It's all yours," Annie said, not wanting to deprive Ethan of a moment of whimsy.

Ethan did as Milo had indicated and squeezed the bear's nose. Seconds later, a drawer at the bear's feet opened, revealing bottles of supplements. Vitamin C. Vitamin D. Iron.

All of them rattled around the drawer, next to similar bottles containing antibiotics and stimulants.

"I'm impressed," Ethan said. "The FBI could take some tips from you."

"Are you admitting to having safe houses across the world? Because I saw that in your files when I was hacking the mainframe a few months ago."

"Again, I'm going to pretend I didn't hear that," Ethan said, taking a seat on the couch.

"Did you find a way to close the loose ends we discussed?" Annie asked Milo, taking a seat next to Ethan and folding her legs with an easy movement.

"Not sure if I closed the loop or opened new ones," Milo shrugged. "But here's what I was able to dig up." He typed into his keyboard with rapid fingers, and images of Riggs— the treasure hunter— popped up on the screen. Newspaper articles about his past finds appeared, along with images of his van. Milo highlighted what looked like a police report, blowing it up to full size. "I've got more on the file that was erased from the Police Database the morning after the murderer."

He zoomed in, making the font bigger.

"Report filed," Ethan read aloud. "Officer observed a brawl at *Feisty Mike's* bar between two citizens— Riggs, and," Ethan paused, recognizing a familiar name. "Paul Kaminski."

"How long ago did the incident occur?" Annie asked.

"Three weeks before the murder," Milo answered. "And then the file was deleted from the Police mainframe the morning after the murder. First that domestic dispute report, now this…"

"Why didn't your time machine catch it on the first go around?" Ethan asked.

"My first search was for Karen," Milo shrugged. "I wasn't even looking for Riggs when I pulled this up. I was doing a search on Paul."

"Does it say what the fight was about?" Annie asked.

"No," Milo shook his head. "Just that it got down to fists and bruises. Seems like other patrons at the bar were able to separate them and call the police before things got too bad."

"Another dispute Karen failed to mention," Annie said thoughtfully. "In fact, none of the neighbors mentioned it. People around here say Paul was a model citizen."

Milo snorted. He noticed Annie and Ethan's curious expressions. "Come on," he said. "People around here stick together. You're not gonna get the real story from any of them. We look out for each other. You two—" He motioned between Annie and Ethan. "You're outsiders. I just happen to like you and consider you friends. But to everyone else? You can't be trusted. Don't ask locals for the real story. Ask other outsiders who've been here longer."

"That's..." Annie chewed on her lip as she thought about what he'd said. "Surprisingly helpful. Thank you."

"Anything on Dr. Burns?" Ethan asked.

"You'll find this interesting," Milo said, typing on his computer again. An application for grant funding appeared on the screen, its lines followed by essay-style responses and graphs outlining where potential funding might go. "Dr. Burns' appeal for grant funding was denied."

"He's not getting any more money," Annie confirmed her suspicion out loud, pleased that it had led to a fact.

"This was an appeal. The original application was denied months ago," Milo said.

"Why would he come out here on his own dime?" Annie wondered. "The hotel fees. The research assistant he has back at the university. All of it costs money. He claimed his salary was robust but his body language said he was lying. Can you confirm?"

"His salary is dismal," Milo answered. "I make more in ten minutes hacking the Treasury than he does in six months of work."

"Didn't hear that either," Ethan said, looking at the ceiling as if he might find a particular interesting spider up there.

"Where's he getting the money?" Annie asked under her breath.

"No idea," Milo said. "But the family might know. On that note, I got you something." He reached into a desk drawer and pulled out two black burner phones.

"Thanks, but we're good," Ethan said, waving a hand in the air. "I had both our phones encrypted by the FBI. They're unbreakable"

Milo snorted, then hit a single key on his keyboard. The screens lit up with images of call logs, both incoming and outgoing, from Annie and Ethan's phones. "Really? You're sure?"

"How'd you—?" Ethan started to ask, alarmed.

"I didn't," Milo said. "I found this while looking for your guy." He leaned in suddenly serious. "I'm down a rabbit hole on your case. This is about more than just locating an IP address. This *Real Estate Ripper* figure goes deep. Real deep. I went through each IP one by one and they were all police station-based, until I found something strange..." He clicked on the keyboard and an IP address appeared on the screen next to a map of Europe. "This one was routed through a proxy serve in Europe." He clicked again, opening up a map of Japan. "Which was routed through a Proxy in Japan." He clicked again, revealing another map, this time of South Korea. "Which was routed through a proxy in South Korea." He typed again, and the screen filled with dozens of maps of various countries. "Three hundred proxies daisy- chained together. I can't tell you the work it took to locate the root IP."

"You did it though?" Annie asked, heart pounding.

"Almost. You won't believe this, but," he paused. "The main address was an alphabet agency." He glanced at Ethan, who currently worked for the FBI. "I'll say which when I know more. I'm trying to get through the door and identify which computer in what segment the source IP came from. In the meantime, you two need to be careful. He's been following your every move." Images appeared on the screens of Annie and Ethan's call logs. "He's been tracing your calls through the satellites to get your location. He knows where you are and who you're reaching out to."

He held out one burner phone to both Annie and Ethan. "So I'll ask again. Sure you don't want these?"

As they reached out to take the phones, Annie couldn't help but notice that Ethan looked particularly bruised by the revelation. She could only hope the alphabet agency in question wasn't Ethan's beloved FBI. He had dedicated his life to the organization. Betrayal from within would crush him.

"I've saved the phone number for Sophia Barnak's family in there and let them know to expect your call. They said they're happy to answer any questions. Don't forget they're on Pacific Time."

"Thank you," Annie said. She stood, feeling it was time to leave. Ethan was looking pale. He could use a cheeseburger.

"Yeah," Ethan nodded, his eyes distant. "Thanks, man."

He followed Annie towards the stairs, pausing at a plate of brownies on the kitchen counter. "You *do* have more than canned beans!" Ethan started to reach for a brownie. "Mind if I—?"

"I don't know bro," Milo laughed. "Those are from Gladys. Not sure you can handle them. She grows a strong strain. They'll rock your world."

"These," Annie said, her mouth dropping open. "These are pot brownies?"

"Edibles," Milo shrugged.

"And you got them... from *Gladys?*"

"Sure," Milo said. "Everyone knows she makes the best cannabis products. Lotions. Edibles. When it comes to weed, Gladys is the original gangster, no cap."

"Nobody told us that!" Ethan said.

"You're not from here," Milo reminded him. "Can't be trusted. Plus, you look like a huge narc."

"Thanks for that," Ethan said.

"Thank you for everything," Annie agreed smiling to herself. "You've been helpful, Milo." She glanced at the brownies, a suspicion brewing. "In more ways than one."

With that, they ascended the staircase, Annie feeling invigorated by chasing a new beat.

CHAPTER NINETEEN
GLADYS

GLADYS HAD DRIVEN her truck to Chesapeake, making sure she wasn't followed. During the drive, she checked her rearview mirror every thirty seconds, and even made a series of unnecessary right hand turns that formed a square to throw off any potential pursuers. She'd made her way to a side road on the perimeter of Chesapeake county, which sat just East of Sunray. Now, she was parked outside the ship-yards, standing outside her truck and leaning on the driver's side door, arms crossed. In the harbor, ships came in and out. Naval ships. Delivery vessels, with enormous containers mounted to their backs. One ship blew a low, mournful horn, and Gladys shuddered at the sound. It felt as if the ship was tattling on her, calling the authorities to intervene in her unlawful activity. Thankfully, she was parked behind a series of warehouses, and no one was around this early in the morning. She was safe. At least, she hoped she was.

There was a crunching sound as four tires moved over the gravel side road and a petite sedan rounded the corner. A "HERTZ" sticker in the window indicated it was a rental car. The door slammed, and the man Gladys was waiting for stepped out of the driver's side:

Dr. Burns stared at Gladys, taking a couple of steps toward her but stopping in his tracks as if he was afraid to get too close.

"This far from town? Really?" He said, his eyes scanning Gladys' confident form.

"You said you wanted to meet," Gladys shrugged. "I needed it to be somewhere we wouldn't be overheard. Assuming you're doing what I think you're doing."

"And what is it you think I'm doing?" Dr. Burns asked.

"Backing out," Gladys said. She clocked his reaction. Dr. Burns' eyes drooped a little, and he fiddled with the cuff on his blazer. Gladys knew she had guessed correctly. "Coward," Gladys sighed. "Why is it that academics can always appreciate the theory of the thing, but not the doing of it?"

"Because in theory, it sounded like a good idea!" Dr. Burns said, his hands rising to his head as if he were about to tear what little hair he had left straight from his scalp. "It's not *technically* illegal— certainly a code of conduct violation that could get me fired, but at least the charges wouldn't be criminal." He paced back and forth, rehashing a conversation he'd had with himself many times before. "But now? There's been a murder! And we have two detectives poking around. They're going to dig up everything. They're going to call the University and tell them the truth."

"Do they *know* the truth yet?" Gladys hedged, hoping Dr. Burns hadn't already done something rash.

"No," he sighed. "But I'm going tell them. Tomorrow morning. I've already set up the appointment."

"I would advise you not to do that," Gladys said, her voice steely and calm.

"Gladys—" Dr. Burns answered, holding his arms out as if he were trying to tame a Grizzly Bear. "This isn't personal. I should never have agreed to accept your payment. My last grant appeal just got denied and I suppose I was hoping on some level that I could accept the money from you, wait for the grant to go through, and cancel the whole exchange once I had proper funding. But now that it's not possible, I have to stop this whole charade—"

"You don't want to do that," Gladys said, almost feeling sorry for the weak opponent in front of her. "You're making a huge mistake."

Dr. Burns moved to the backseat and pulled out a black duffel bag. He unzipped the top, revealing wads of cash tied up with rubber bands. He stepped toward Gladys and dropped the bag at her feet like he was making an offering to a mob boss.

"It's all there," he said. "You can count it. It's all in cash just like the first time so there's no record of the exchange. I had to take an advance from my credit card but I don't care. I just want out."

"Once you're in, there's no out," Gladys sighed. "You're going to regret this."

"I'm sorry, Gladys," Dr. Burns answered. "But I have to get ahead of this. If I tell the detectives the truth and cooperate with the investigation, maybe they won't inform the University of what I've done and I can go back to my average life."

"You're going to mention me by name then?" Gladys asked.

"I believe I have to," Dr. Burns said, his face etched with regret. "They're going to want to know everything. This is my only way out. Begging for mercy and being cooperative. There's no other chance."

"*This* is your last chance," Gladys said. "Stick with the plan. Stay the course. We're so, *so* close."

Dr. Burns appeared to consider her offer, but then, fear flashed across his face as he thought of what he stood to lose. "I'm sorry, Gladys, but—" he looked at the ground, then back up at her. "It's over."

With that, he hopped back in the driver's seat of his rental car and reversed over the gravel road, making his way back onto the main street and disappearing from view. The black duffel bag of cash sat at Gladys' feet. She looked at it with disdain.

Gladys had always felt that only locals could be trusted, and Dr. Burns had just proven her right. At least in Sunray, the residents had each others' backs. They had *loyalty*. This was why Gladys always tried to deal with people she trusted. She'd taken a risk, trusting Dr. Burns— an outsider. Her plan had been a good one. Her only mistake had been placing her confidence in someone who didn't belong in Sunray.

Gladys sighed and picked up the duffel bag, shoving it in the trunk of her car. She wasn't worried— instead, an icy calm pulsed through her veins. Dr. Burns would regret double-crossing her.

All she had to do... was activate the phone tree.

CHAPTER TWENTY

THE MOTEL ANNIE and Ethan had chosen to stay at was located halfway between Sunray and Chesapeake. The building was the only structure around on the edge of a long, empty road. In the dark of the night, its wooden frame blended in with the landscape behind it, creating a camouflage effect. Only the motel's blazing neon sign that flashed "VACANCY" stood out in the sea of black.

In a lower floor room, Annie and Ethan lay in bed, their arms around each other. On a modest television set, a late-night show blared. Ethan ran his hands through Annie's hair. She rested her head on his chest. A host on the show made another joke. Neither Annie nor Ethan laughed. Annie knew they were both using the show for background noise— their minds were elsewhere.

"Do you want to talk about it?" Annie asked, glancing up at Ethan.

"He can't work for an agency," Ethan answered. "Milo thinks he knows, but he could be wrong."

"Milo's never wrong," Annie countered.

"He's just a kid," Ethan shrugged.

"Milo's *never* wrong," Annie repeated. She flipped over to

look at Ethan's face, resting on her forearms and pulling the blanket closer over her shoulders. "There's some good people who work at the agencies," she began.

"You're looking at one," Ethan said.

"I agree. There's good people who work at the agencies—and *bad* people. There are good people in prison. There's bad people who are judges, who are lawyers."

"I get the point," Ethan answered. "Doesn't make it easier."

"I know," Annie sighed. "This is why we rely on facts, not suspicions." She paused, looking out the window. They'd left the blinds open because their room faced the back of the motel, which had nothing to offer but an empty field. Outside, grass blew in the wind and far-away lights twinkled, indicating a town in the distance. "I guess you have to decide... do you care enough about the truth that you're willing to risk learning something you don't want to know?"

"It's been so long since I saw her," Ethan said, thinking about that last moment he'd seen his sister before she'd disappeared for good. "The picture they used on those *missing* posters? I keep superimposing it onto the way I remember her. Like I'm just remembering the idea of her in the press instead of who she really was. Isn't that terrible?"

"It's not," Annie said, her voice a whisper.

"Sometimes I wonder if I should just let go," Ethan said, glancing out the window at the dark, open field outside their room. "I spent all this time building up a life I thought would honor her. Now, I might have to give it up to find her."

"Don't rush to conclusions," Annie said. "We don't know yet. Suspicions aren't facts. You're thinking twelve steps ahead."

"Sound like anyone else?" Ethan laughed.

"I might *guess* twelve steps ahead but I don't conclude so far in advance," Annie shook her head.

"I prefer to leap into things," Ethan said, pulling her closer to him and wrapping his arms around her. "I leaped into loving you and I don't regret it yet."

"Give it time," Annie smirked.

Ethan stared at the ceiling, considering his career with the FBI. He'd proven himself again and again. Getting a job with an alphabet agency had required top grades in school. Athletic ability. Countless hours of training. "I joined because I thought they'd give me a family I could count on. One dedicated to making sure other people wouldn't have to go through what we did. One with *loyalty*."

"Loyalty," Annie repeated, ambient light from the television screen casting blue and yellow shadows across her face. "They certainly have that here in Sunray, don't they?"

"You think so?" Ethan asked, suddenly curious. He could tell when Annie was circling a theory about a case.

"More loyalty than I've seen in a long time," Annie nodded. "It's making things difficult. But I also admire it. It's hard not to admire people who keep their word. That stick together." She intertwined her hand with Ethan's, wondering what it would do to him if he was forced to leave the FBI. There'd been so little Ethan could really count on in life. Annie was determined to be the kind of person who would never let him down.

She looked out the window again, staring at the lights in the distance. The people of Sunray could count on each other. And knowing who to count on was half the battle in life.

CHAPTER TWENTY-ONE

RIGGS

IT WAS EARLY when Annie and Ethan met Riggs for another interview. The morning sun was just breaking over the horizon, its rays turning the landscape orange and pink. Riggs waved at them from the edge of a small field he was standing at, a baseball cap sitting cock-eyed on his forehead.

"Come on over," he shouted, motioning Annie and Ethan towards him. He stood next to his van— Seth by his side— the backdoors open and a whirring sound echoing from within.

"Up to no good this morning?" Ethan asked, taking a sip from the paper coffee cup he was holding.

"Like always," Riggs joked.

"The LIDAR machine again?" Annie queried, peeking at a set of computer inside the van. Overhead, the scanner attached to the roof made a beeping sound as it completed another circle.

"Right you are," Riggs agreed. "This is our last area to scan and then we'll be about done here."

"Thanks for meeting with us again," Annie said, leaning against the van. "I've had a couple of questions pop up since our last meeting and I wanted to run them by you."

"Shoot," Riggs said, taking notes on a pad as data from the scanner lit up the computer screen in the back of of the van.

"Why do you scan so many areas if Sophia Barnak's property is the only one the diamond might be hidden on?"

"Seth, you take this one," Riggs said, nodding at his partner, keeping his eyes fixed on the screen.

Seth cleared his throat. "Well, it's about the probabilities. Land shifts over time, especially with natural events like flooding or fire. Then you add in the fact this is all farmland, and there's quite a bit of runoff from all the irrigation. It's reasonable to be concerned that something buried might move to adjacent properties."

"These are hardly adjacent properties though, are they?" Annie asked, motioning at the empty field in front of them, which was at the edge of Sunray's Western border. "We're quite a distance from the corner store."

"Well, that's the second point," Seth continued. "We go to a lot of different areas, and we always make sure to map the entire district in case at some point a private buyer wants to purchase the scans from us. The LiDAR technology itself is expensive and hard to come by and we're one of the only small companies that offers it in a transportable form. You know, given Riggs' invention..." He pointed at the scanner that was attached to the roof of the van.

"What kind of private buyers would want to buys something like that?" Annie asked.

"Real estate developers," Riggs offered, cutting in before Seth could answer. "Climate change specialists." He paused, remembering his last interview with Annie. "I believe we've answered this question before."

"Of course," Annie smiled. "I supposed what I was really asking was... do you have a buyer right now who's interested in the scans?"

For the first time, Riggs looked away from the screen and

stared at Annie, concern etched in his features. "We don't comment on ongoing deals," he offered.

Annie's face said she took that as a "yes."

"No problem," Annie said, taking a step back. "I just have one more question."

"I'll try to have one more answer," Riggs said.

"During your time on the property, have you stopped by the corner store at all to look at the interior?"

"Just once," Riggs shrugged. "Paul allowed us access to examine the building."

"But not since his death?"

"Nope," Riggs said.

"I just wondered because we stopped by earlier today and the place had been ransacked. It was almost like someone went in there and tore it apart because they were looking for something."

"Seems like a bad way to look," Riggs shrugged, comfortable with the lie. "I can tell you— it wasn't us. We have processes for these things. Methodology. We try to leave things the way we found them. We don't just go rob a place like tomb raiders."

Seth couldn't help but let his eyebrows raise— that was *exactly* what they'd done. Annie didn't miss the look that crossed his face.

"The wallpaper was pulled down," Annie continued. "And what was funny about it was I'd noticed the wallpaper myself the first night was saw the place. It was smooth on every wall except for one. Almost like somebody had pulled just that piece down and put it back up. Funny, isn't it?"

"Strange," Riggs agreed. "Wish I could offer some more information, but the family really preferred us staying outside on the grounds."

"Oh!" Annie said, pretending to slap her forehead. "Funny you should mention that. We spoke to the family and they said they didn't seek you out."

"Pardon?" Riggs asked, leaning against the van with a wounded look as if Annie had slapped him. "What are you implying?"

"Nothing," Annie said innocently. "Just that the family said it was actually *you* who came to *them* asking to investigate the claim of liquid gold."

"That's possible," Riggs shrugged. "We have so many important hunts I forget who came to who. Might've mixed this situation up with another one. It happens."

"Sometimes," Annie smiled at him. "Well, thanks for your time. We'll be in touch."

She took a final sip of her coffee as her and Ethan headed back toward their rental car. As he watched them walk away, Riggs couldn't ignore the sinking feeling he was running out of time.

"We need to wrap this up," Riggs muttered to Seth under his breath. "Get out of town."

"I'm ready when you are, boss," Seth answered.

Riggs didn't want to tell Seth that this was one adventure they wouldn't be taking together. A small piece of Riggs had dreamed of staying in Sunray, but now, his mind spun as he began making plans for his escape. His heart pounded as he considered one churning, important detail:

There was something Sunray offered him that he'd never found anywhere else.

And he didn't want to leave— without her.

CHAPTER TWENTY-TWO
VERONICA

VERONICA HEADED for the home of the one person she knew she could count on. At least, a person she was *pretty sure* she could count on. She was in the front seat of her cherry red Hyundai sedan— a used car she'd bought in high school that was on its last leg. Veronica had forced the car to continue operating long past the moment it had lost the will to live, mainly because she couldn't afford another one.

It's all going to be okay, she told herself. *This can be fixed. You have help. She loves you and would never betray you. It's going to be okay.* She fiddled with dials on the dashboard, trying to turn the air conditioning lower. Luke-warm air blew back at her— evidence that the AC was next to quit.

There was a backfiring sound as the car rolled up a long, dirt road, landing at Gladys' house.

Veronica visibly relaxed as she stepped out of the car, her shoulders lowering. She stomped up the porch like she owned the place and opened Gladys' front door without so much as a knock.

"Come on in," Gladys shouted from the sitting room.

Veronica entered, finding Gladys seated at the kitchen table, a notebook open in front of her. It was such a comforting, familiar sight that Veronica resisted the urge to cry. Her eyes welled up despite herself.

"Oh, stop your tears," Gladys clucked. "It's going to be just fine. Understand? I just thought it was time to talk about the thing rather than running around what we both know is a problem."

"You said you wanted to talk to me," Veronica said, shaking although she tried to stop it. "I *knew* you knew this whole time. And now you're going to say something aren't you? You're going to tell everyone what I did. I don't blame you, Gladys. I really don't."

"I'm not going to say a thing," Gladys sighed, patting the seat beside her. Veronica took the seat, crossing her hands over her legs. "If I were going to squawk, I would've done it by now. Do you really think I'd do that to you, child?" Gladys continued. "Hush. Although I believe I *did* tell you not to take the job selling the farm. Didn't I say this was one you would regret?"

"You did," Veronica said. "You should know it wasn't totally my fault—"

"'Course it wasn't," Gladys agreed. "Women have it so hard. A man makes a mess and you're left dealing with the pieces. I knew it the moment I saw you."

"I just needed the job," Veronica cried. "It's my first one. How could this happen on my *first one?*" She groaned, putting her head in her hands.

"Well, it *has* happened now," Gladys offered practically. "And what's done is done. I didn't invite you to have a talk to pressure you, and I'm not going to rat you out, no matter what you decide. All I'm suggesting is that maybe it's time to take some action over hiding. Aren't you tired of hiding?"

Veronica nodded. "I really thought I could matter," she said, wiping her eyes. "I just wanted to be the best real estate agent the state had ever seen. And now, it's all ruined."

"You can still be whatever you want," Gladys said. "But there's someone we need to talk to first."

Veronica's eyes widened as she realized what Gladys was suggesting.

"No, I can't—"

"You *must*," Gladys said. And just like that it was decided. "Come here," Gladys wrapped her arms around Veronica, who melted into her embrace. "You're going to face this problem head-on and eradicate it so it doesn't come back to bite you in the ass later on. Hiding doesn't do anything. You hear?"

"I hear," Veronica agreed. She knew Gladys was right. She'd been running away from this for too long. It was time to take action. "What do we do?"

Gladys smiled. She had a plan— and it was a good one.

CHAPTER TWENTY-THREE

KAREN

HOURS LATER, and Karen knew everything. She was seated at her kitchen table, Gladys and Veronica across from her, nursing two cups of tea in wildly different mugs. Gladys' eyes were uncharacteristically wet. Veronica's cheeks were flushed. The two women were a mess.

They both stared at her, waiting for her to say something.

"That's it, then?" Karen said. She had heard the entire story and had little to offer in the way of a reaction.

"That's it," Gladys confirmed. "You know it all."

"Just fine then," Karen nodded. She turned the teacup around in her hand, looking at the pattern on its side. "Do you all like my cups?" She asked, motioning at the colorful mugs in their hands.

Veronica's eyebrows arched in surprise. "Karen, I don't think you understand what I've just told you! I'm saying that—"

"She understands what you're saying," Gladys clucked. "She's got ears, doesn't she? A perfectly operational brain as well, I assume Karen?"

"It's all working fine as far as I know," Karen agreed, tapping her temple.

"See," Gladys nodded, satisfied. "Karen understands *exactly* what you said. She just happens not to care much. Isn't that right?"

"Wouldn't say I don't care at all," Karen shrugged. "But I understand why you did it. There were many times I could have done the same. Almost wish I had. But now... this has all worked out rather well for me."

"That— that can't be true—" Veronica sputtered.

"And why can't it?" Gladys smiled. "Karen's been quite busy with her recent adventures, haven't you Karen?"

Karen gave Gladys a warning look. "*Private* adventures, yes," Karen said. She cleared her throat. "What Gladys means is I've been remodeling the house. Brightening things up a little."

"I liked the green color you painted the foyer," Veronica offered weakly, letting her head fall into her hands. "This is such a mess," she said, wiping snot from her nose. "Such a mess." She looked at Karen again. "I'm so sorry. I'll never be able to set this all straight."

"Not quite," Gladys said, slapping a notebook on the table. She opened it to a page that outlined a list of phone numbers, full names and addresses next to them. "I think all it'll take is a bit of elbow grease. The phone tree's gotten pretty long over the years, but with the three of us, we'll get through it just fine."

"The three of us?" Veronica asked, surprised.

"You didn't think I'd help?" Karen said, shaking her head. "Honey," she reached a hand across the table and placed it over Veronica's hand. "I babysat you when you were three years old. You brought me that soup when you were a teenager and I had my hand surgery, do you remember?"

"Of course I remember," Veronica said. "It's just— your *husband—*"

"Was as useless as they come," Gladys said. "More trouble than he was worth."

"A right old donkey," Karen agreed. "The point is, I've known you all your life. We do things our own way around here, and I understand exactly what brought us to this moment better than you know. We don't need anyone else meddling in a situation that's none of their business. So..." she paused, glancing at the phone tree. "I'll start with these pages," Karen said, ripping a few sheets of the phone tree from Gladys' notebook.

"And I'll take these," Gladys said, ripping additional pages from the book to place in front of her. She passed the remainder of the phone tree to Veronica. "The rest is yours."

"What do we say?" Veronica asked, her face still flushed. "How do we make everybody understand without telling them everything?"

"All we need," Gladys smiled. "Is the perfect patsy. Someone who's an outsider. Someone who isn't one of *us.* And I've got a prime candidate..."

"I just need to be done by seven," Karen said, twirling a piece of hair around her finger. "I've got... *plans.*"

Gladys gave a disapproving snort, which Karen pointedly ignored. The three women picked up their cell phones and began to dial, activating the phone tree with the force of a natural disaster— unstoppable and irrefutable.

Gladys couldn't help but smile. Dr. Burns was going to regret double-crossing her.

CHAPTER TWENTY-FOUR

DR. BURNS

DR. BURNS HAD CHOSEN to meet Annie and Ethan at a neutral place. Specifically, he'd selected the town's only diner and was now seated at a booth in the back, a plate of hash-browns and eggs in front of him. Overhead, a light fixture flickered. Outside the diner's windows, the dark, night sky made the neon signs of the few businesses on this street look like neon buoys on a black ocean.

"... and once my grant got denied, I realized my only way out was to tell you everything," Dr. Burns said, pushing the hash-browns around with his fork like they might be the last he'd ever eat. "So here I am, ready to tell you everything."

"Sounds excellent!" A cheerful voice answered. Annie was seated across from him, Ethan by her side. They had just finished two cheeseburgers, and their postures mirrored one another. They both exhibited a strange cheerfulness that made Dr. Burns feel all alone in the world.

"You're prepared to hear what I've done?" Dr. Burns asked, a little surprised at the levity they brought to the moment. "I've never confessed to a crime before. I didn't expect it would feel so... welcomed?"

"We love it when people confess," Annie shrugged, her

shoulders moving toward her ears as if they were trying to cast off any bothers. "Typically we prefer when they confess to murder, but I know that's not where you're headed. So I'll settle for whatever it is you have to share."

"Right, well," Dr. Burns cleared his throat. "You're correct in that it's not *murder*. I didn't kill Paul. Although if I did, I wouldn't tell you. So just out of curiosity, what makes you so sure it's not me?"

Annie stirred the straw in her fountain soda, a faraway look in her eyes. "Because somebody else did it," she said, as if he'd asked the stupidest question she'd ever heard. "The evidence is obvious, but I do have some loose ends to tie up. I'm afraid the identity of the killer only gets clearer as time moves on."

"Oh," Dr. Burns considered, glancing at Ethan. "Do *you* know what she's talking about?"

"No idea," Ethan said with a smile. "But I've learned to just go with the flow."

"Interesting," Dr. Burns said, stroking his chin. He'd suddenly begun to feel he'd made a terrible mistake deciding to confess his sins. If Annie already had a suspect in mind and that suspect *wasn't* him, he might be better off keeping his mouth shut. "You know," he said, stretching his arms wide. "I've actually just realized how busy you two are, what with solving a murderer. And what I have to say was so minor... it might be better for me to head back to the inn rather than distracting you with petty crime..."

He started to stand but Ethan stood as well, blocking the exit to the booth, arms crossed.

"We'd still like to hear what you had to confess," Annie offered congenially. "Even if it's minor, it might help with the investigation. Besides, I'd like to wrap up every mystery here, and your mere presence in Sunray has been quite strange, to say the least."

Dr. Burns sat, defeated. Ethan returned to his side of the

booth and the three of them were cozy in their places once more. Now that balance had been restored and Dr. Burns realized he had no direction to head in but forward, a calm came over him. It was now or never. He took a deep breath and began to tell the truth.

"I accepted money from a resident of Sunray in return for conducting my research here," Dr. Burns said. "This resident, I believe, came by the funds illegally."

"Most excellent," Annie said, happy that this news was consistent with her current theory on who had murdered Paul Kasinski. "Go on?"

"The University of Virginia prohibits me from engaging in privately funded research without going through the proper channels," Dr. Burns said, a guilty look flashing across his face. "But I couldn't resist. My grant had been denied. No one sees the value anymore in investigating the formation of immigrant communities! They don't understand that accessing our past is the key to unlocking the present—"

"It's a shame," Annie nodded, although the urgent tone of her voice indicated she didn't care about society's heinous disregard for history. "So you accepted payment from a resident of Sunray to conduct research on the area's history?"

Dr. Burns nodded. "I thought I could use private funds to get the ball rolling and then bill it back once I received a proper grant approval. You have to believe me, I'm genuinely interested in safeguarding the historical resonance of this incredibly unique community—"

"I believe you," Annie assured him. "A key question remains: why would this resident want you to research Sunray, and be willing to pay a hefty sum to boot? What was in it for them?"

"I wasn't asked not to research Sunray in particular, although of course I conducted a thorough study of the area as a whole, otherwise my research would be meaningless and unpublishable." Dr. Burns pushed his glasses higher up on his nose. "Instead, this person wanted me to study the Sophia Barnak store specifically."

"To discover what?"

"Whether it could be counted as a landmark via Sunray's Historical Society."

"Is that a difficult status to get?" Ethan asked.

"Yes, actually," Dr. Burns reached into his briefcase and fished around within, extracting a paper that he passed across the table. "You have to meet all of these standards." He leaned over his dish, pointing out the bulleted items on the page. "Item one... The property must have original significance to the settling of Sunray prior to 1930. Item two... The property must have a current standing in near original condition. Item three... there must be sufficient documentation provided to corroborate the property's standing as having historical significance..."

"Quite the laundry list of items," Annie noted. "And you have to prove all of this to get historical standing? I can see why the person who hired you wanted an expert."

"I've spent so much time at the property, photographing the corner store. I've been to the library, the courthouse— I have hundreds of pages that we attached to the application."

"So it's done then?" Annie asked. "You've applied?"

"Certain documents have alluded me," Dr. Burns sighed, ashamed to admit he was a failure even at this simple task. "Namely, the original deed to the property proving Sophia Barnak's ownership at the time. There was no history of the document at the local library or the courthouse. I had told Paul as much the night before he died, hoping he might encounter it in the corner store or through the family out West. And then when he was murdered, I paused my research."

"And why's that?" Annie crossed her arms, inferring she already knew the answer.

"Because I was worried the murder was connected to the

person who hired me. You see, the person who hired me was desperate to stop the sale of the property from going through. And she thought that getting the property declared a historical landmark would slow down the process."

"Why would that slow down the sale?" Ethan asked.

"Because you can't *build* on a historical landmark, isn't that right?" Annie said. Dr. Burns offered the slightest nod in confirmation. "A historical landmark must remain intact, and all buildings have to be maintained in their original condition. Historical societies can place a litany of provisions on property owners. In some places, you can't even change a fence outside a historical landmark. So a buyer wouldn't be able to tear down the corner store or construct a new building on the land. They'd have to purchase it as-is. Which greatly narrows the field of potential prospects."

"It does," Dr. Burns agreed. "I thought it was quite clever, actually, that she came up with such a plan."

"And that brings us to our final question?" Annie smiled. "Who was it that hired you to research the Barnak property?"

"She'll cause hell when she finds out," Dr. Burns said, his arms shaking a little. "People are quick to write her off but the woman is practically a mob boss."

"I need to hear you say her name," Annie answered.

There was a long pause, and then Dr. Burns said the name Annie had been hoping for:

"Gladys."

CHAPTER TWENTY-FIVE
VERONICA

IT WAS late in the evening— or early in the morning, depending on how you looked at it— by the time Veronica, Gladys, and Karen finished activating the phone tree.

They were halfway through the list when Karen excused herself to go meet up with an unidentified person. She scooted her chair back and said, simply, "Time for me to go, ladies."

"We can take this over to Gladys' house…" Veronica said, holding up the piles of pages with phone numbers on them that had been scattered over the table.

"Nonsense," Karen answered. "You stay right here until you're finished. This is too important to interrupt." She shot a knowing look at Gladys. "If you leave before me, just make sure you close the screen door. Betty's taken to coming inside uninvited. Scared me half to death the other night. I woke up with her looming over me, practically trying to climb into bed with me."

"Will do," Gladys assured her. "Have fun. But not *too* much fun."

With that, Karen had slipped out the kitchen door, leaving Gladys and Veronica to finish calling the remaining numbers. Hours ticked by with ease, and before Veronica knew it, they were all the way through the phone tree. When the work was finished, they had locked the screen door as Karen requested and waved goodbye to Betty, who was asleep in the fields.

Now, they were sitting on Gladys's front porch, eating two of her famous brownies together.

"These get better every time you make them," Veronica said to Gladys, looking out at the corner store on the lot next to them.

"That's just because I increase the strength," Gladys said, wiping her mouth and taking another bite.

"No," Veronica chewed slowly. "It's the chocolate. It gets better with every batch." She paused, lost in thought. "And actually... what *is* chocolate?"

"Isn't it a bean?" Gladys answered.

"A cocoa bean," Veronica agreed. "But if chocolate is a bean, why doesn't it *taste* like a bean?"

"Maybe all chocolate is a bean but all beans aren't chocolate," Gladys offered helpfully.

"Kind of like all murderers are people, but all people aren't murderers," Veronica said, leaning back on her elbows so the warm breeze blew over her face. "Murderer. That's an awfully big word, isn't it?" Veronica started to reach for another brownie, but Gladys removed it from her hand with the quick movement of a practiced expert.

"No more for you," Gladys said, taking a bite of the brownie herself. "You're starting to creep me out. That's when it's cut-off time."

"Whatever you say," Veronica shrugged. "Do you think less of me?" She asked very suddenly, her eyes watering.

"Of course not," Gladys answered.

"I just wanted to make something of myself," Veronica said. "To be more than the sum of my parts. To be a bigger somebody than what I started as, and to matter to the world around me in a way that's undeniable. I wanted to do something *special*. Do you think that's so bad?"

"Not bad," Gladys said, recognizing the folly of youth. When she'd been younger, she'd wanted so deeply to stand out. Later, age had taught her life wasn't about standing out — it was about being the most authentic version of yourself a person could be. "Just a little off the mark. You'll understand what you're really trying to say when you're older."

"Is Karen seeing somebody?" Veronica asked. "She had that vibe about her like she's found somebody who looks at her the right way. You know what I mean when I say the right way?"

"Sure do," Gladys acknowledged.

"I hope I find somebody who looks at me that way one day. Hell, I hope I look at myself that way one day. But it's always the wrong person, isn't it?" Veronica thought aloud, wondering at all the wrong people she'd met in her life thus far. "Why is it *always* the wrong person?"

"Beats me," Gladys said, kicking her feet up on the stairs. "But I reckon they're all wrong up until the right one."

"Wooooah," Veronica sighed, her eyes widening. "That was so deep." She paused, imagining Karen out in the world with a mysterious man who looked at her just the right way. She pictured the two of them holding hands, just gazing at each other, sitting in the middle of a field like they were the only two people on Earth. "If Karen *is* seeing someone, I hope it's the right one."

"Oh," Gladys sighed. "I highly doubt that."

"Why?" Veronica asked.

"Because," Gladys said. "He's not one of us. He's from out of town. And you know how that always goes."

Veronica nodded. She knew exactly how that went.

"Then it's destined to fail," Veronica agreed. "Guess that's why she doesn't want anybody to know, then?"

"That, and the fact she's married," Gladys answered.

"Oh yeah," Veronica giggled. "I always forget about Paul. But I guess I won't be able to now." Her face suddenly dropped like she'd remembered a bad dream she'd had from the night before. "Not for the rest of my life. Never, ever, not so long as I live will I ever be able to forget him—"

Suddenly, Gladys took Veronica's face in her hands, gripping it as if her cheeks were a bird that might take off in flight. "Now, you listen to me," she said, a serious blade hovering in the reflection of her eyes. "You never let a man dictate the course of the rest of your life. If the roles were reversed, do you think he would be considering you every night forever? Do you think he considered *your* feelings at all that night, or just himself and what he wanted in the moment?"

Gently, Veronica shook her head to indicate she didn't think he would be pondering her existence very hard.

"Damn right, he wouldn't. Paul would be thinking about himself right now, and his next move. That's what you're 'gonna do, honey. Think about your next move."

"My next move," Veronica repeated, massaging her cheeks now that they were free from Gladys' grasp. She leaned back on her elbows again, looking up at the stars. There were too many to count this time of year, and they seemed to outnumber her in a way that was reassuring— like each star was the possibility of a better future, if she could only be brave enough to take it.

CHAPTER TWENTY-SIX
RIGGS

RIGGS KNEW it was going to be a good night. He was sitting on the hood of his van, where he'd constructed a temporary roof-top deck. A warm blanket and two pillows leaned up against the structure. The van was parked in an open field, pointing toward a water tower. It was a simple view, but it made Riggs feel connected to something bigger than himself. He'd been surprised to find that smaller-town living gave him the same sense of connection that came with hunting antiquities around the world. Riggs had always thought he needed to see the world to be a part of something, but since arriving in Sunray, he'd been made aware of a new way of living. Sunray had taught Riggs that adventure alone wasn't enough to sustain a life. It was *love* that made life worth living.

And Riggs had found his own love.

At that exact moment, her perfect figure became visible in the distance. She was his age, and stunning. Long hours managing the farm had made her strong and virile. The slice of the life she'd experienced thus far made her more full of wisdom than any artifact he'd pulled up from the dirt.

There she was, smiling at him: Karen Kaminski.

Never mind that she was Paul Kaminski's wife. Small details like marriage or commitment had never bothered Riggs. He'd been around the world enough times to know that only two things mattered: what a person was willing to do to get what they wanted, and who they took with them on the trip.

No, it never bothered Riggs that Karen was married to Paul. He'd barely considered the other man when he'd made his move that first night he'd met her, when he'd come to ask her what she knew about the neighboring property of Sophia Barnak's store.

He remembered the moment clearly. He'd knocked on the screened-in front door, expecting to see a bored housewife answer. Instead, Karen appeared in the doorframe, and Riggs' heart skipped a beat.

One thing led to another, and he asked her if he could take her to the local bar for a drink under the guise of "picking her brain" about the farm.

She agreed, and it was there— sitting at a table over the sawdust-covered floor— that Paul fell in love with her. He learned about Karen's passion for art, and how her husband had smothered it out of fear she might leave him. He listened to her stories about the sculptures she'd made and the art history degree she'd obtained but never used besides teaching the occasional summer-school class. Paul shared his own tales of finding art across the world, buried in sand and under the sea.

Karen stepped toward him and kissed him, hard. That was another thing Riggs loved about Karen. She was all rough edges and soft landings, able to present two opposing forces at the same time.

"Missed you," Karen said, smiling at him as they parted. "But only a little bit."

There it was. The fact that she wanted him, but didn't *need* him. Yet another reason Riggs had fallen for Karen.

"I made us an evening," he said, taking her hand and leading her up the steel ladder that ran vertically up the length of the van. She climbed it rung by rung, gasping as she reached the van's roof and spotted the makeshift viewing area Riggs had created. Plush pillows offered an invitation, and twinkling lights offered a romantic effect.

"Guess you kind of like me then," Karen said.

"I like you so much I have a proposition for you," Riggs answered, leaning back on his arms and looking up at the stars. Karen nestled her head onto his shoulder, and he knew — this was the moment he'd been waiting for. "I found it," he whispered into her sweet-smelling hair.

Karen sat up with a jolt. "No!" She exclaimed, flipping over to look at him more closely. "The treasure?"

Riggs nodded. He reached underneath one of the pillows and pulled out a simple file folder. He passed it to Karen, who opened it up, her eyes widening in shock. "It's— this is it?"

"I thought it would be the diamond, but I had it wrong, Karen," Riggs said, excited to finally be able to share what he'd learned. "*Plynne zloto*, liquid gold. It wasn't the diamond at all. It was—"

"I see now," Karen nodded, staring at the papers in the file. "What are you going to do with it?"

There was a pause as Riggs took her hands in his. "I'm going to run," he admitted. "And I want you to come with me. Tomorrow. I've already chartered a plane. We take it and get out of town, preferably out of the country. We can buy new identities. Erase my past so we're free to travel. We can start over, together. Maybe some place by the ocean," he added, looking out at the vast sea of inky, night sky on the horizon. "I can hunt for shipwrecks and you can work on your sculptures. It'll be a brand new start. We could even tie the knot, if…" Riggs paused, feeling suddenly vulnerable. "…If that interest you."

Karen blinked away her surprise. She'd settled in Sunday a long time ago, and had never imagined living anywhere else. What Riggs was offering was a fantasy. But Karen had learned from experience that fantasies often turned out to be just like anything else in life— complicated. Paul had started out as a fantasy, and look at how that had turned out. He had promised her safety and security. Instead, Paul had brought her pain and insecurity. How could she be sure Riggs wouldn't turn out to be the same kind of man?

"What about Seth?" Karen said, referencing Riggs' partner as she tried to buy time to think. "Won't he want a cut?"

"Seth," Riggs waved a hand in the air. "He got paid for his time. He's not entitled to anything, but if you want to feel good about it all we can wire him some money abroad once we get there." Riggs kissed her, pressing his lips to hers as if the action would wake her her up. "Karen, honey, this is it. It's everything we've ever wanted sitting right in front of us, but we have to leave tomorrow. Those detectives are poking around. If this comes out, there'll be fights over ownership. Disagreements over who's entitled to what. It's time. All you have to do is say *yes*."

Karen stared at him, unable to believe where she'd ended up in life. All she'd ever wanted was a good husband, a safe house, and an honest living. Now, she'd emerged with a dead husband who was never good to begin with, an excellent lover, and the opportunity to be independently wealthy. Life was funny like that. It reminded Karen of the sculptures she made. They started out as nothing but a heap of clay, but by the time she was done with them, they were birds in flight or women holding jars. Maybe this was her chance to try something new.

Karen chewed on her bottom lip for a moment, then said the word she'd been too afraid to say up until this point:

"Yes."

There. It was done. She kissed Riggs under the stars, and told herself that no matter where she was going— whether the experience turned out to be a dream, or a nightmare— at least it would be a big adventure.

CHAPTER TWENTY-SEVEN

DR. BURNS

IT WAS two in the morning when Dr. Burns had the strangest dream. He dreamed that he sat up in bed and opened his eyes, startled awake by the noise of the door to his hotel room being thrown wide open. Sheriff Chomski stood in front of him, gun drawn, two cadets from the Virginia State Troopers by his side. In Dr. Burns' dream, Sheriff Chomski read him his Miranda Rights as the state troopers cuffed his arms behind his back, pulling his from his bed in the most undignified way. Somewhere in the chaos, Dr. Burns was sure he had heard Sherriff Chomski say he was being arrested for the murder of Paul Kaminski, which was an amusing muddling of facts, given that Dr. Burns had never touched Paul. Dr. Burns found it fascinating that his brain would connect a nightmare to something from his daily life, like the investigation at the Barnak farm. What a marvel, dreaming was!

During the nightmare arrest, Dr. Burns was clothed only his striped pajamas, which had shrunk in the wash and were much too small for him, exposing his ankles to the elements. The troopers had hauled his shocked, limp body into the hallway and out of the Bed & Breakfast, shoving him into a

Police Car like a sad piece of luggage. In the dream, Dr. Burns had only blinked his eyes over and over, aware that he was dreaming and marveling at the strangeness of it all. He didn't try to intervene or stop the process, if only because that was the way dreams were to be handled— it was best to sit back and enjoy the ride, assured by the guarantee that one would wake up shortly having ridden out the worst of it all.

Dr. Burns waited to wake up, but the moment never came.

It wasn't until he was sitting at the Sheriff's station in Sunray's only jail cell that Dr. Burns began to realize none of this was a dream at all. He really *had* been arrested. He really *was* in handcuffs, his right arm linked to the steel bench he was seated on. All of this was real, and Dr. Burns was in a very large amount of trouble.

Struck by the strangeness of it all, Dr. Burns felt his breathing quicken, and he did something he had never done once in his life: he prayed.

As an academic, Dr. Burns had always preferred to focus on what was tangible and provable, mainly because he worried believing in anything else might subject him to the derision of his peers. But now, sitting in a jail cell with absolutely no idea how he had ended up there, Dr. Burns succumbed to the natural human inclination to connect with the beyond. He prayed in rambling sentences, none of them making much sense, except for one he repeated over and over again:

Please, send someone— anyone— to help me.

It was just then that the door to the Sheriff's station flew open, and a figure stood framed in the doorway, the breaking light of dawn encasing her in a golden glow.

I've been sent an angel, Dr. Burn's thought.

Instead, Annie Hudson stepped forward, her hands on her hips and her head tilted to the side.

"Do you make it a practice to arrest innocent men or only when *I'm* on the case?" She asked Sheriff Chomski, a humorous glint in her eye. Behind her, Dr. Burns recognized Agent Ethan Beckett, the man who was always at her side.

"Now, Annie," Sheriff Chomski raised his hands in the air, standing up from his desk like he was afraid she might try to take him to task. "We have reasonable evidence. More than a dozen eye witness accounts saw Dr. Burns leaving the property the night Paul was killed."

"Interesting," Annie nodded. "I don't suppose they all happen to be members of the phone tree?"

Sheriff Chomski sighed. "Annie. Sunray is a small place. Everyone is a member of the phone tree."

A voice piped up from the second desk in the Sheriff station. It was Sheriff Chomski's daughter, Stacey, holding a coffee cup and sitting in her rolling chair. "Dad," she said, garnering her father's immediate attention. "Milo says they're the best. If Annie doesn't think Dr. Burns killed Paul, we should listen to her. I want this over as much as you do," she stood, touching her father's arm. "I know, it's stressful. But we can't let an innocent man take the fall for something he didn't do just because it's easier for us."

Sheriff Chomski looked at his daughter like she'd just been born once more. Children were like that— always changing in ways you hadn't seen coming. Unruly, like flowers that choose to grow on the garden fence instead of the trellis positioned by a careful gardener. The pleading look in her eye was one he'd seen many times before— one that was impossible to ignore.

"We'll release him on his own recognizance for forty-eight hours," the Sheriff sighed, placing his hands on his belt loops to show he meant business. Stacey clapped her hands together and threw her arms around her Dad's shoulders. "But I want him back here before the clock runs out," the Sheriff said to Annie and Ethan. "And if you haven't offered me a new suspect by then, well—"

"I believe we can solve the case by then," Annie nodded cheerfully. "We only have a few loose ends to tie up."

"We do?" Ethan asked, surprised. He'd had no idea Annie was close to solving the case. But that was how Annie worked — in a silo, her genius mind sorting through facts to find relevant truth.

"We do," Annie confirmed. "Stacey? Would you like to do the honors?"

Stacey took the key from her Dad's belt loop and approached the only jail cell in all of Sunray. Dr. Burns blinked again, unable to believe his prayers had been answered, if not quite in the way he expected. There was a clanking sound as Stacey unlocked the cell and moved Dr. Burns' handcuffs, her father standing nearby, arms crossed in a watchful, imposing posture.

Dr. Burns stood, emerging from the cell a changed man. His prayer had been answered, and he'd been given a new lease on life. His guardian angel for the day— Private Investigator Annie Hudson— put a well-meaning hand on his shoulder. "Don't worry," she told him. "We're going to set this right. In the meantime... you look like you could use a cheeseburger."

CHAPTER TWENTY-EIGHT

AFTER TREATING poor Dr. Burns to a cheeseburger and interviewing him one more time, Annie and Ethan set off to tie up what Annie called "loose ends." They hadn't learned any new information that was particularly exciting from Dr. Burns, except that he was now a man of faith and was thinking of leaving academia to join the church. Now, as their rental car sped along a dirt road toward Sophia Barnak's farm, Ethan couldn't help but smile.

"Seems like Dr. Burns is leaving one group for another," Ethan said. "First he was in the religion of academia, which he viewed as infallible. Now, he's moving on to actual religion."

"Point being?" Annie asked, her arm resting on the edge of the open window, the world rushing by in a blur of green and brown.

"I guess I'm just thinking that if he can do it, I can do it," Ethan shrugged. "If Milo tells us the Real Estate ripper is connected to an alphabet agency, and I decide I have to leave the FBI on principle, I'm capable of starting over with something else."

"You're capable of anything," Annie said, putting a hand

on his knee. The one good thing that had emerged from her traumatic past was her relationship with Ethan. Annie had resisted the connection at first, but now, she knew he was always meant to be her silver lining. And she was done running from the past. *"We're* capable of anything," she added. "If we have to start our own vigilante alphabet agency with just the two of us to start with, that's what we'll do."

Ethan winked at her. "I like the way you think."

The car pulled up to the familiar exterior of Sophia Barnak's farm. Annie and Ethan exited, stepping onto the land with a renewed sense of justice. Annie was close to solving the case, and she could smell the answers on the air. She just needed to verify her suspicion with a fact.

"Let's start at the back of the farm," she said, motioning for Ethan to follow her to the area of the farm furthest from view, arriving near the edge of the dismal swamp. When they reached the spot, it was freshly tilled, a small, brown fence that had been there days prior now removed as if it had never existed. Annie smiled, bending down to touch the soil.

"Do you remember what was here the first day we saw the farm?" She asked Ethan.

"Nope," Ethan shrugged. "But I know you do."

"Pot plants," Annie said. "I didn't mention it to anyone because I know it's illegal to grow cannabis in Virginia. They were hidden back here to try to keep them from view. I hoped the answers would emerge eventually, and they have."

"Gladys," Ethan nodded. "Wouldn't have put my money on that one."

"She tried to destroy the evidence," Annie agreed. "But she's too late. There's only one more thing we need to do before we close the case."

"What's that?" Ethan asked.

"I want to speak to the couple that was leasing the land from the family before they decided to sell it."

"We'll get Milo on it," Ethan agreed.

CHAPTER TWENTY-NINE

HOURS later and Annie and Ethan were sitting inside an ocean-side condo located in Virginia's Chesapeake Bay, adjacent to the naval ship-yard. Milo had secured contact information for the brother and sister pair that rented the property prior to the family's decision to sell, and the siblings had been more than happy to accommodate a brief meeting.

Ethan stood at a pair of glass sliding doors that gave way to the ocean-view balcony, looking out at the bay. "It's nice that the ocean is so close to Sunray," Ethan said, more to himself than anyone else. "When I think of a farm, I never assume it will be by the water."

"We're trying to talk Ethan into a quieter life," Annie smiled from the couch, taking a sip of her glass of water. Across from her sat Melissa Davies, one half of the sibling pair that had purchased the farm. Next to her was her brother, Joshua Davies, and Annie couldn't help but marvel at how alike the pair looked. Melissa was in her late fifties with raven-black hair and wide eyes. Her older brother was balding, but what little hair he had left told Annie it was the same color.

"Sunray is certainly quieter," Melissa volunteered. "At

least up until now, what with this whole murder business. The two of us grew up out there and left for a time to live other places. Then Joshua got divorced—" she nodded at her brother, who pursed his lips together as if he wished she hadn't shared so much about him. "And I got laid off. So, we headed home and tried to see if anyone needed some help while we both got back on our feet and saved some money. Running Sophia Barnak's farm was a God-send for us both. We're doing better now. Got this condo and some money saved."

"I took a job on an oil rig," Joshua offered. "So I travel half the year. Helps that I won't be around too much to drive my sister crazy."

"When you were running the farm, did you notice anything strange about Paul? He was your neighbor at that time, correct?"

The siblings exchanged a glance. Melissa leaned in. "Look, the problem with Paul is he's a downright menace. No one will tell you as much because people like to keep their problems close to the vest in Sunray, especially when it comes to outsiders. But now that we've left, I guess we can say whatever we want. Isn't that right, Josh?"

"Damn straight," Joshua sighed, putting down his cup. "People act like Paul is a pillar of the community just because he's done some local volunteering and is great neighbor. Willing to help anyone with anything. Except for when he's drinking, in which case— well, I wouldn't want to be his wife, Karen."

"Did you see fights between the two of them?" Annie asked.

"Sure, even broke up a couple," Joshua nodded. "We were sleeping in the corner store at the time so we heard it all. We knocked on Karen's door but she never took the help. Paul got in fights around town, too. Never with a local— he was too smart for that. He knew the community would intervene.

But anyone passing through could expect to be on the wrong side of Paul if they crossed paths with him."

"And, this may be a touchy subject..." Annie said, shifting in her seat uncomfortably, "But— did you allow anyone to grow cannabis plants on the property?"

The siblings looked as if they'd been caught in a criminal act, both their wide eyes getting even wider. Ethan took a seat on the couch, offering a reassuring posture. "This is all off the record. We only care about solving the murder. The pot plants are gone now, so what do we care?"

"You're with the FBI, you said?" Joshua asked, suspicious.

"I am," Ethan admitted. "But I'm starting to wonder what that even means." There was a pause as he considered. "I care more about the truth than anything."

"We let Gladys rent part of the farm from us to grow her plants," Melissa said, blurting out the words as if she'd been holding onto them for too long and couldn't wait to release them. "We weren't supposed to sublet, and we didn't tell the family out West about it. But we needed extra money, and Gladys needed a place to grow her product that gave her plausible deniability if she were caught." A wistful look came over Melissa's face. "And her brownies were so good. Have you tried them?" Annie and Ethan shook their heads in response. "They'll take the edge right off whatever you're going though, and hell, we were both goin' through something."

"And what about the treasure?" Annie asked, cutting right to the point. "Did you ever find anything on the property?"

"Nope," Joshua said. "But Paul believed it was real. Soon as we were gone and the family hired him to oversee the place part-time, he was raring to go, looking for that treasure. Silly fool."

"Thank you," Annie said, standing. She had received all the information she needed and was excited to see the case to its conclusion. "You've made an innocent man very happy."

"Will you tell us who did it?" Melissa asked, an edge in her eyes. "We miss the local gossip, to be honest. We get updates in the group text chat but it's not the same. This will give us something to talk about for weeks."

"You can count on it," Annie smiled at her.

CHAPTER THIRTY

KAREN

KAREN HAD NEVER BEEN on a private plane before. The fact struck her as she stood on the tarmac at Chesapeake Regional Airport, her shoes sticking to the asphalt. She gazed up at the small, private plane that was parked in front of her, its wings stretching out to the side like appendages on an insect. Not only had Karen never flown in a private plane, she also hadn't flown much at all. She could remember twice in her life she'd been up in the air. Once, she'd flown an hour to visit a cousin up North. The other time, she'd been to New York to see a play. Both times, she'd made sure to have a stiff drink before take-off, and had gripped the seat the entire flight. Now, she was about to get into a small, metal death trap for many hours. She wondered if private planes were any less safe than commercial flights. She figured they must be, as commercial flights were held to the highest standards of safety and governed by regulatory agencies.

"He's about to get the engines up," Riggs said, appearing at her side. He'd been inside, talking to the pilot they'd chartered. "He says we can board anytime."

"Where did you find this guy again?" Karen asked, trying

to sound nonchalant about the idea of leaving everything she'd ever known behind.

"Hired him off an app," Riggs shrugged as if the means of hiring were of no consequence at all. "This is just a puddle jumper. Let's get our asses out of Virginia. He'll drop us off in Florida, and then we can catch a connecting flight out of the States."

Karen gripped the handle on her suitcase a little tighter. Her palms were suddenly sweating, and she felt a bit woozy. "And, um," she asked, trying to keep the details of their plan straight. "Once we leave the United States we're going… where?"

"Anywhere you like!" Riggs exclaimed, throwing his hands up in the air. "London, France, Italy… I might have to stop by Brazil before we get to our landing spot, though. I know a guy there who can get us fake I.D.s. He helped me get a false permit to lift treasure from the coast of Montenegro and let me tell you, the guy is good."

"*Montenegro*?" Karen breathed the word out like a sigh. She realized she had no idea where Montenegro was. Was it a country? Or a city? In fact, Karen wasn't well acquainted with Europe in any way. She had studied European Art as part of her degree in Art History, of course, but it had all been in the abstract. She'd relied on photographs and Google searches. Never had she actually traveled there to see the items in person. The idea sounded exciting, but maybe more so with a tour guide and an officially sanctioned visit.

She stared at Riggs, realizing that as much as she'd enjoyed his company, she wasn't sure she really *knew* him. He talked about fake documents as if procuring them was nothing but an inconvenience. A minor obstacle to be over-come rather than an international crime.

The problem was, Karen loved Riggs. She really did. But she wished everything was happening the right way.

It was then— on the sticky tarmac, feeling all alone in the

world— that Karen did something she hadn't done in a long time.

She prayed.

She asked God to put her in the right place at the right time and to somehow make all of this work out. She asked creation itself to tell her which way to go, and to make the choice for her, because she had no idea what to do, and her suitcase was suddenly very heavy. If she declined to get on that plane, she might lose the only man she'd ever really loved. But if she went with Riggs, she'd be sentenced to living a life that was perhaps… *too* exciting. Too dangerous.

In that moment— much as Dr. Burns had done in his small jail cell— Karen prayed and turned her future over to the one that had made her, trusting in the divine order of things. She begged God to make the decision for her. If she wasn't meant to go, let the plane fail to lift off. If she *was* meant to go, she asked God to move her forward when her own legs would not listen.

"Ready?" Riggs asked her, a big smile on his face. He reminded Karen of a little dog, enthusiastic and eager. He meant no harm. He just leaned into the adventure of life, and it never occurred to him that Karen might struggle to do the same.

"I—" Karen started to answer, but just then, her prayers were answered.

"Hands up!" A shout came from behind them. Karen whirled around, surprised to see a guardian angel:

Annie Hudson.

Her hands were in her pockets, Agent Ethan Beckett by her side. On her other flank stood Sherriff Chomski, gun drawn.

"Sherrif Chomski?" Karen said, sure she must be dreaming. The man she'd known since Kindergarten was slapping handcuffs onto Riggs.

"Sorry about this, Karen," he said. With that, he pulled her own hands behind her back, cuffing her wrists. "It's just—you might try to run. And we need everyone in one place to explain."

"Explain what?" Karen asked, having completely forgotten about the murder investigation. For now, she was simply relieved she didn't have to get on that plane.

"Paul's murder," the Sherrif said, his eyebrows raising in surprise. "She solved it. Annie solved it."

Karen shot a sidelong glance at Annie, who was smiling at her with no ill intent. Karen bit her tongue, resisting the urge to say, "*Oh, is that all?*"

She allowed Sherriff Chomski to escort her into the back of his cruiser, relieved that— no matter what happened from here on out— her prayer had been answered, and she was never, ever, getting on that little plane.

CHAPTER THIRTY-ONE

BY THE TIME the group was assembled at Sophia Barnak's farm, it was mid-day, and the sun cast its rays upon the crowd with magnificent force. Ethan couldn't help but think that the heat reminded him of Annie and her intensity— the scorching clarity of vision she possessed that had brought them all together in this very moment. At least one hundred people had congregated outside the corner store, shielding their eyes from the sweltering day, baseball caps pulled low in defense. It seemed as if the entire town of Sunray had decided to attend today's festivities.

"I'm sure you're all wondering why we've brought you here," Annie shouted to the crowd. She was positioned in front of the corner store and was standing on a stray bucket to make herself visible to the collective.

"You're 'gonna tell us how Paul died!" A voice shouted from the back of the crowd.

"That's exactly right!" Annie agreed. "Except, of course, most of you already know how Paul died, because you called the Sheriff's office and claimed you saw Dr. Burns exiting the corner store immediately after the murder. Correct?"

Murmurs scattered throughout the crowd. The wave of

whispers, as if Annie had run through the crowd in her underwear by mentioning the unmentionable.

"In which case you'd have no reason to be here, given that you already know the truth. And yet, here you all are— the people that saw Dr. Burns leaving the farm, eager to hear who committed the murder. Strange..."

Beside Annie, Gladys rolled her eyes. She wished she could control the stupidest of her peers, but alas, not everyone had a mind as sharp as hers. Next to Gladys was the entire group of potential suspects: Veronica, sweating in one of the ridiculous work blazers she insisted on wearing even though she wasn't showing a single property that day. Next to Veronica was Dr. Burns, still in his striped pajamas, looking equally as ridiculous in clothes that didn't fit, his bright, white ankles exposed for all to see. Beside Dr. Burns was Karen, her arms crossed, and next to Karen stood Riggs in a similar position, his eyes scanning the landscape as if he might find a path through which he could make his escape. Finally, at the end of the lineup stood Agent Ethan Beckett and Sheriff Chomski, both of them keeping one hand on their weapon, prepared to pursue any suspect who tried to vacate the situation.

"Now that we have *that* out of the way," Annie continued, let's discuss how Paul Kaminski might have actually been murdered. It's clear that the dozens of calls from the community claiming Dr. Burns was at the corner store that night were made in bad faith. In fact, it's almost as if someone activated the phone tree and asked its members to report a false story. Isn't that right, Gladys?"

"I am unable to comment on the activation of the phone tree, given that it exists only for members of Sunray and not *outsiders*," Gladys responded in a huff.

Annie nodded, pleased, almost as if she'd hoped for such an ornery response. "I certainly understand," Annie continued. "While it is false that Dr. Burns committed the murder, the callers were actually onto something. You see, while Dr. Burns is not the killer, he *was*, in fact, engaged in some elicit activity." She turned to Dr. Burns, an encouraging look on her face. "Would you like to share what you did with the group?"

"I accepted payment to study Sunray," Dr. Burns shared. "A resident here hired me to try to prove that Sophia Barnak's farm and corner store had historical value. You all have a unique history here, given that this area is one of the first and most extensive Polish immigrant settlements in the United States. Given that Sophia Barnak was one of its key founding members, along with her husband, Frank, the land has distinct historic appeal. She provided a key service running the corner store, and after Frank's death, was one of the earliest female business operators in the county." Dr. Burns seemed to brighten for a moment, and suddenly the fact that he was a Professor became very apparent. "Did you all know that Sophia's husband's mother, Mary Barnak, was one of the first Poles to arrive in Sunray? She came over with a mere hundred dollars in her pocket and came right here to form what would later become Sunray..."

"While I'm sure the crowd is very interested," Annie cut him off. "Perhaps we could save that for a book you'll write in the future?"

"Of course, of course," Dr. Burns agreed, a little embarrassed at how excited he'd become to share his love of history.

"Can you tell the crowd *why* the individual that hired you wanted you to prove this farm's historical standing?"

"The person that hired me wanted me to get the Sophia Barnak Farm and Corner Store admitted into the historical society so that a sale would become more difficult," Dr. Burns answered.

"Yes," Annie agreed. "This person wanted to ensure that the land would become ineligible for development via its historical status. Because, you see," Annie turned to the crowd as if she were a magician about to reveal the secret of her trick. "Once a structure is declared a landmark via the Historical Society, that structure is prohibited from being demolished or destroyed. Such a status would make Sophia Barnak's Farm & Corner Store less appealing to potential buyers... including developers."

Annie didn't miss Veronica's wide-eyed look. It was as if she were piecing something together, a hint of betrayal in her eyes.

"And who was it that hired you?" Annie asked Dr. Burns.

"Gladys," Dr. Burns shrugged.

The crowd gasped, whispers working their way through the group.

"Hogwash," Gladys said. "Who would believe him? He's not one of us. We can trust a thing he says."

"Perhaps we can trust what we know of Gladys, then," Annie continued, pleased to have Gladys' assistance in making her point. "We know that Gladys loves Sunray. She has access to the phone tree, and is a leader in the community. We also know that Gladys makes the world's finest brownies."

A hush fell over the crowd. It appeared the subtext of Annie's comment was not lost on the group. Based on the crowd's reaction, many residents of Sunray had enjoyed Gladys' products.

"The brownies required a special ingredient Gladys could not grow on her own farm out of fear of being implicated. Gladys, isn't it true you used a piece of land at the back of Sophia Barnak's farm near the dismal swamp to grow your cannabis plants, which you sold in various baked goods, soaps, and lotions?"

"I won't answer that without a lawyer," Gladys replied.

"Regardless, I'm sure many here would be willing to testify to the truth of your activities," Annie continued. "Returning to what we know: we can be quite certain that Gladys hired Dr. Burns to research the Sophia Barnak Corner Store and Farm in order to collect the necessary evidence to have the property admitted into the historical society. Her motivation for doing this was to stop the sale to a developer. A deal in-progress which she would have been aware of thanks to the Real Estate agent on the project, Veronica."

Annie turned to Veronica, whose eyes were wide. She looked as if she might cry. She glanced at Gladys, betrayed.

"I told you I was reaching out to developers! How could you?"

"Now listen," Gladys held up her hands. "I know you have big dreams for Sunray, but I told *you* this place was meant to stay in the hands of people who know what it means to be a local resident. You young ones always want to go changing things that are best left alone—"

"But that wasn't the only reason you wanted to stop the sale, was it Gladys?" Annie asked innocently. "You wanted to give your cannabis plants more time to sprout. You'd gotten used to using the land for free, and needed time to make another plan." Annie allowed her eyes to scan the line up of suspects, considering her next move. She paused when her gaze landed on Karen, standing next to Riggs. "And Gladys wasn't the only one making plans. Isn't that right Karen?"

"I suppose we're caught now, aren't we?" Karen turned to Riggs, regret etched in her eyes. "There's no more running from it." She turned back to Annie, her posture that of a fox caught in the teeth of a coyote— limp and resigned. "Riggs and I were planning to leave Sunray. We've been having an affair."

The most outraged gasps so far circulated throughout the crowd. The idea of murder and weed was one thing, but an affair was truly juicy gossip.

"How did you know about us?" Karen asked Annie.

"The mug that you had on your counter. That wasn't a mug at all. It was a Native American ceremonial bowl. Quite an impressive find, in excellent condition. It belongs in a museum somewhere, but given that it was sitting on your kitchen counter, it was likely gifted to you by an unscrupulous trader. Perhaps one banned from travel and stuck looking for artifacts in the United States."

"It's true," Riggs admitted. "I gave it to her. And I'd do it again a thousand times." He eyes burned as he looked at Karen. "That asshole didn't deserve her. Paul didn't know what he had—"

"Ah, yes, and that brings us to Paul. The man himself was quite a mess, wasn't he? You all told me he was a pillar of the community, but that was hardly the truth, was it? The Police Reports showed otherwise. It seems Paul had been in multiple altercations, including domestic disputes with Karen and a fight with Riggs at a local dive bar. All this occurred among many other infractions. Strangely, we had to have a friend dig up the truth, as the records of Paul's outbursts had been buried."

Annie glanced at Sheriff Chomski, who coughed to clear his throat. "Well, our record-keeping isn't great around these parts—"

"It's fine, Sheriff, you don't have to cover for me," Karen said. "I asked him to do it. I didn't want you to think Riggs killed Paul, and I didn't want news of what he did to me getting out." She looked out the crowd. "You all knew he was a scoundrel, but what you didn't know is he was the worst at home."

The crowd fell silent. This news was unwelcome, but not surprising.

"So Paul was *not* such an upstanding member of the community," Annie agreed. "And when he died, you were glad to see him gone. You already had a lover on the side, and Paul's murder simplified things. Didn't it?"

"For the first time in a long time, I felt like I could be myself," Karen answered, her eyes flooding with tears. "The house was mine. My life was *mine*. I was glad somebody killed him. But I didn't do it."

"No," Annie agreed. "You didn't kill your husband. We'll get to that. But first, let's talk about the supposed treasure. Riggs, you came to Sunray because you heard rumors of a treasure on the farm. You told Ethan and me that the family out West hired you, but a quick call with them informed me it was actually *you* who sought *them* out. So... I must ask... how did you learn about the alleged treasure at the farm?"

Riggs sighed. "Seth and I keep a pulse on internet chatboards for treasure hunters, looking for anything that might give us a lead. Paul posted to one of the sites we monitor, asking for advice. He explained Sophia's claim that she hid something on the farm, and when we traced her lineage and the term "liquid gold," we thought he might be onto something. So I scooped the lead. I called the family and got their blessing to take on the hunt. Can't say Paul was happy about it."

"No, I'm sure he wasn't," Annie said. "Given that you were about to board a plane with Karen to leave the country, I can assume you found what you were looking for?"

Riggs nodded. "Liquid gold," he said. "It wasn't the diamond or treasure at all. It was stock certificates."

"Yes," Annie agreed. "I noticed the Coca-Cola signs across the store's walls. I supposed Sophia invested in the stock early on, then?"

"She did," Riggs answered. "And she hid the certificates behind the wallpaper in the corner store. She said she 'buried' it because the print on the wallpaper was of a mountain and trees."

Sheriff Chomski searched Riggs' bag and removed a pile of papers in a folder, holding up the stock certificates for Annie to view.

"And what are these stock holdings worth today?"

"About twenty-five million dollars," Riggs said, his voice heavy with the knowledge he would never see a cent of the money. "Give or take a million," he added.

The crowd gasped, and there were some hoots and hollers from various residents of Sunray who thought that amount of money sounded pretty good.

"The family, who are the rightful owners of the stock, will certainly be happy to hear that!" Annie exclaimed, clapping her hands together. "What a wonderful decision they made, hiring you."

"Best decision," Riggs said, practically spitting the words out.

"Sheriff Chomski, Ethan can make sure the family gets those..." Annie gestured to Ethan, and Sheriff Chomski passed the stock certificates to him like a live grenade. Riggs let out a groan as he watched the papers disappear, as if seeing them leave his possession was physically painful.

"Don't worry, Riggs," Annie smiled at him. "I'm sure you'll still get a payout from your other side deal. The one with... Veronica?"

Veronica stared at Annie, looking as if she'd been caught in the middle of a crime.

"I didn't—"

"You asked Riggs to scan all of Sunray with his LIDAR device to provide developers with a map of the area. It's been your dream to see a more urban, gentrified community, isn't that right?"

"It's not a crime to ask someone for radar scans," Veronica said, adjusting the edge of her blazer.

"Entirely true!" Annie agreed. "And I suppose the interested party that was about to make an offer on the property was a developer. Something no one in this town besides you actually wants?"

Veronica nodded.

"So then, we return our attention back to the wallpaper," Annie said, pacing as her mind ran through the details of the investigation. "Riggs, when you found the stock certificates, had Sophia hid anything else behind the wallpaper?"

"Some meaningless stuff," Riggs shrugged. "Papers from Poland. Personal documents. We threw what was left in a pile."

"Did it look like anyone else had discovered the secret of the wallpaper prior to your arrival?"

"Actually, yes," Riggs said, surprised. "There was one wall where it had already been peeled back. Whatever was underneath had been taken."

"Yes," Annie nodded. "On our first day inspecting the corner store, I noticed a piece of wallpaper peeling from the corner, and was bothered by the ripples in the texture. Whoever peeled it down failed to put in back up properly, and— unlike the rest of the store— the wallpaper on this singular wall was uneven."

Annie turned to Veronica, whose arms were shaking. "Veronica? Would you like to tell us more about that?"

"I just wanted to do something great," Veronica said, her voice a whisper. "He came at me— accused me of things— I was afraid and it all happened so fast."

"Paul found something in the wallpaper, didn't he?"

Veronica nodded. "He'd been drinking. He was obsessed with the idea of the treasure. We were fighting about it because every night he'd go out and dig holes on the land. I was trying to keep everything nice for showing, and he was destroying the place!" There was a pleading tone to Veronica's voice, as if she desperately wished to be understood. "We were always at odds about the sale," Veronica continued. "Paul hated me just because the family hired me to sell the place. He was supposed to be a temporary caretaker for the farm, but then he got so caught up in the idea of finding the treasure. Then when Riggs showed up, his behavior got worse. The night he died, I stopped by the corner store to check on everything..."

"And you walked in on Paul, ripping down the wallpaper," Annie nodded. "What had he found there?"

"He found the deed to to the land, showing its original formation with Sophia and Frank Barnak as the first owners."

"Dr. Burns," Annie said, turning to her friend in pajamas. "Was there anything missing in your research that prohibited you from filing for the Historical Society sooner?"

Dr. Burns went white as a sheet. "In fact there was," he agreed. "I told Gladys I needed proof of ownership. I checked every local records hall and hadn't been able to find anything tying Sophia to the deed."

"And Gladys," Annie nodded at Gladys, who looked as if a truck had hit her. "Did you share that information with Paul?"

"I—" Gladys stammered. "Oh my God. I hadn't thought of it until now but, I did. Paul and I both wanted to stop the sale. Him for the treasure, me for my... *crops.*" She stared at Veronica, horror crossing her face. "I had no idea he would take it out on you, honey. If I had known I would have never said a thing—"

"But he *did* take it out on you, didn't he Veronica?" Annie asked. "You arrived at the store that night and found a drunk, belligerent Paul, waving the deed in your face."

"He was so angry," Veronica answered, her face wet and flushed with the memory of that night. "He came at me and started shouting that I wasn't going to sell this place. He said he had everything he needed. Then he through a jar at me. He tipped over one the shelves. He grabbed my hair and threw me down and— I don't know what happened— I just— I lost it."

"Your instinct to protect yourself kicked in," Annie said.

"I killed him," Veronica confessed, sobbing. "I didn't mean to, though. I grabbed the first thing I could think of. There was a shovel leaning against the wall, probably from Paul digging holes. So I grabbed it and I hit him over the head with it. Maybe harder than I meant to... I just wanted to buy myself time to get away, but— he fell over and, that was it.

He was dead. There was nothing I could do. I panicked and I ran back to my car."

"What did you do with original deed to the property?" Annie asked.

"I took it home and burned it," Veronica answered, ashamed. "I know it makes me look bad, but I just didn't want anything that could stop the sale getting out. And Paul was already dead and I just— I grabbed it—"

"She's not the only one to blame," Gladys said, her lower lip trembling. "I should never have tried to meddle in the sale. And I knew Veronica was the culprit and kept it quiet. I saw her leave and I didn't say anything because, well, if it was any one's fault it I knew it had to be Paul's. If you're going to arrest her, you might as well arrest me." Gladys stepped forward, putting her own body in front of Veronica's.

"I knew too," Karen sighed, stepping forward. "Veronica told me the whole story and I'm, well, at this point I'm probably an accomplice."

"Yes," Annie smiled. "I assume the three of you cooked up the phone tree to falsely accuse Dr. Burns."

"Thanks a lot, Gladys," Dr. Burns scoffed, then muttered under his breath, "Can't wait to get out of this town."

"That's thing about a small town, isn't it?" Annie agreed. "People really stick together."

"Am I going to prison?" Veronica asked, glancing at Sheriff Chomski, her voice shaking.

"Well," Annie offered, "This is quite the complicated situation because— although I may have my belief about what happened— I also have dozens of reports that claim Dr. Burns was seen leaving the property. And I *think* I heard Karen say she was an accomplice. Is that correct, Karen?"

Karen glanced at Annie, reading something in her eyes.

"Yes," Karen said. "Actually, I wasn't just an accomplice," she stepped forward, puffing out her chest. "*I* killed Paul. I killed him myself."

"Oh dear," Annie said, smiling. "It seems the situation has just became even muddier. Is there anyone else who thinks they might have killed Paul?"

"I killed him," Gladys said, raising a hand. She laced her other arm into Veronica's in a show of solidarity. "I hit him over the head, hard. With a shovel. I did it that night and I would do it again."

"Oh no," Annie shook her head in mock dismay. "Now this is really an unsolvable situation. Did anyone else kill Paul?"

"Ah, hell," Riggs said, stepping forward. "I killed him. We had a fight in the bar and I was screwing his wife so I wanted him dead. I hit him in the head with a shovel. Killed him good."

"Anyone else?" Annie shouted at the crowd, opening her arms. Voices echoed from the crowd as citizens of Sunray stepped in to protect their own.

"I killed Paul!" A plump man in the back shouted, raising his hand in the air.

"No, *I* killed Paul," An older woman laughed, clutching her handbag closer to her body.

"No, it was me," Milo shouted. He was in the middle of the crowd, holding hands with Stacey. "I killed Paul!"

"No, *I* killed Paul..."

"— No, it was definitely me who killed Paul—"

The crowd devolved into a flurry of conversation, each person trying to claim credit for the murder.

Dr. Burns cleared his throat and stepped forward, whispering in Annie's ear. "I just want to be very clear that my official stance is I did *not* kill Paul."

"Noted," Annie assured him. She raised her arms high in the sky. "Well, it seems that we simply have too many confessed suspects to make sense of this case! Sheriff Chomski, how do you feel about marking this one unsolved?"

"I think it's the only way forward," the Sheriff smiled at her. "And I'm glad to see you're doing things our way."

"Not all outsiders are bad," Annie smiled at Gladys. She looked at her lineup of suspects one more time, thinking about how people could at once be each other's biggest problem, or their greatest solution. Dr. Burns bounced on his heels, eager to get home and away from Sunray. Gladys and Karen had their arms around Veronica, reassuring her that all would be well. And Riggs stood next to Karen, looking utterly lost, like he would never be sure what to do with himself again.

"Where are we going to go?" He said vaguely, staring at Karen. "The money's gone. We can't travel. What should we do?"

Karen smiled at him, kissing him like it was the first time. "Maybe we'll stay right here for now," she said, looking out at her neighbors in the crowd.

Riggs nodded, agreeing. "You know, I like it here more every day."

And with that, the case was solved.

CHAPTER THIRTY-TWO

THE CROWD LINGERED for some time after the case was resolved. Neighbors clapped each other on the back, proud to have pulled such a clever stunt off together. Hugs were given to Veronica, who had become a local legend as the murderess set free. Annie couldn't help but think that Veronica's real estate business was likely to do much better due to the publicity. The knowledge that Paul had harmed Karen seemed to have made him an outsider in the town, and Veronica was crowned a new neighborhood hero. All in all, the community of Sunray had done what they had always done— they had stuck with their own, deciding to succeed together rather than fail alone. Annie thought back to Dr. Burns' description of the original Polish settlers in the area, and she saw the way in which their resolve, fortitude, and commitment to each other had lived on in their ancestors that made up the present-day town.

From the crowd, a figure emerged. It was Milo, carrying a large backpack on his shoulders.

"I think you made Stacey love me even more than she already did," he said to Annie, nodding at Stacey, who was standing next to her father, Sheriff Chomski. "She's so relieved her Dad doesn't have to be stressed out by this. Now that everybody knows what happens, it's a chance for a new start."

"We can all use one of those," Annie agreed.

"Speaking of," Milo said, looking around as if he was worried someone might overhear him. "I found your guy."

Without meaning to, Annie reached over and grabbed Ethan's arm, clutching it tight in her hand as if she might fall over without his help.

"To what degree of certainty?" Ethan asked.

"One hundred percent," Milo offered, a sad look in his eyes. Milo opened up his backpack and extracted a file, which he offered to Ethan. There was a quiet in the air as Ethan accepted he documents, feeling as if both his and Annie's lives might change forever.

"You have no idea what this means to us," Annie said.

"Your guy works for an alphabet agency, but it's not the FBI," Milo stated. "It took work to get to the bottom of it, and I had to hack multiple firewalls, but I was able to trace to initial request for data to a desk at a building that's listed online as being vacant."

"Trade craft," Ethan confirmed. "The building won't exactly show up on Google Maps."

"It didn't," Milo agreed. "So I had to use data from a Russian satellite, which showed me an image and gave me the exact coordinates. I also hacked Kremlin files that revealed the building is a known CIA black site."

"I didn't hear that," Ethan said sternly, although by now, Milo had so charmed him that it was difficult to keep the smile off his face.

"It gets weirder," Milo offered. "The computer I tracked the request to requires an individual login token. I was able to track the token to one user. A man named Russel Grey."

"What do we know about him?" Annie said, her detective's mind already on the move.

"What we know is he's a trippy dude. He was a criminal profiler for the C.I.A. Specializes in psychology and willful manipulation of an asset's cognitive faculties."

"Mind control?" Ethan grimaced, reading from a page in the file in his hands.

"Dude was into some weird stuff," Milo said. "But the strangest part is that he's off the grid now." Milo rifled through the file in Ethan's hand, stopping when he reached a particular page. "Here. He quit the C.I.A. and moved to a commune out in the hills. Who knows what he's doing out there."

"Well," Annie turned to Ethan, a twinkle in her eye. "I've been looking for a new adventure. A little break from the world. How about you?"

"No," Ethan said, horrified, his mouth dropping open. "First a farm, now this? What if they don't have a Cheesecake Factory—"

"Milo," Annie reached out and shook his hand. "Thank you for your help. You have no idea how much we appreciate you."

"No problem," Milo agreed. "What're you guys 'gonna do now?"

"I think," Annie said. "We need a change of pace."

Ethan sighed. "Seems like it's time for me to grow out my beard, Milo. If Annie has her way, it looks like we're joining a commune."

"Hey, man, you've already been in a cult if you were with the F.B.I.," Milo patted Ethan on the back. "You'll do great out there. Lots of practice."

"No," Ethan shook his head. "I'll do great out there because I'm part of the right team." He took Annie's hand in his. "We won't have the F.B.I's support on this one," he said to Annie, concerned. "Think we can get by without it?"

"Definitely," Annie said.

"Hey, woah!" Milo waved his hand in front of their faces

as if he were trying to wake them up from a dream. "You guys didn't think I would bail on you now, did you? You can count on me for remote tech support, no questions asked."

"Milo, I can't let you do that," Annie said. "It's too dangerous."

Milo rolled his eyes. "In case you have noticed, we stick together around here. You're part of Sunray now, and we take care of our own. Whether you like it or not, I'm here for you."

"It may not be as flashy as the F.B.I.," Annie said to Ethan, "But I'd bet on our team."

"Me too," Ethan agreed.

Annie inhaled deeply, letting the warm scent of the afternoon linger in her lungs. This place would stay with her, wherever she went. The people of Sunray had taught her that choosing the right community was everything. And Annie?

She'd picked a partner she could count on.

———

To stay on the case with Detective Annie Hudson, look for "Murder in the Commune,," Book Four in the Private Investigator Annie Hudson Series.

Keep reading for an excerpt from "Trail of Obsession," Book One in the Predator / Prey Thriller series!

TRAIL OF OBSESSION
CHAPTER ONE

I'M NEW, the world is infinite, and my life will always be made of beginnings.

The words tumble through my brain as our little Subaru zips up a snake of a road, weaving its way toward Yosemite. Pristine, crisp air glides over the silver hood, four new tires bouncing on uneven pavement. Mike wanted to rent a Prius and I wanted an SUV, so we met in the middle. Compromise. A thing I'm learning to live with.

Mike glances at me from the driver's seat.

"It has more get up and go than you thought, right Zoe?"

"Maybe," I shoot back, pretending to check the dashboard. "Are you happy with the gas mileage, mister environmentalist? If not I'll pop open the floor hatch and we can Flintstone our way up the mountain."

"Not in these shoes," Mike grins, opening up the external vents, filling the car with the scent of pine trees and possibility. It makes my head swim, heavy with the promise of an outdoor adventure.

The passenger-side window glides down with ease when I press the automatic button. I un-click my seatbelt, sticking my upper body out the window.

Sheets of green whiz by; dense forest spiraling into forever. I've always loved the wilderness, if only because it's a place where no one expects anything of you.

In my day-to-day life, I'm a hotel manager, and the job requires me to focus on appearances. We're an upscale establishment. Chandeliers trickle from the hotel ceilings like sticky icing on the side of a cake. Walls covered in dense floral wallpaper muffle the secrets of our guests, framed by drapes so soft you could fall into them and never find your way back out again. It's all about decorum, there, and it takes a special kind of person to do the job. Ninety percent of my time is spent addressing grievances with, "We're sincerely sorry for that, ma'am," and "Apologies, sir." The other ten percent involves smiling even though I want to smack someone. But none of that matters out here, in the wild. The forest doesn't care if I'm rude, or dirty, or a beast. She only cares that I show up.

My fingers turn white, gripping the hard edge of the window. My head tosses back, and my lips form a perfect "o" as I howl into the infinite everything.

"Watch out everybody, she's on the prowl," Mike reaches for the back of my jeans and puts a hand on my ass, and I whip around like a dog who doesn't like his tail grabbed.

"You better watch it."

"Or what?"

"Or I'll bite you." I kiss his neck— reckless— not caring that he might take his eyes off the twisting mountain road. It's been too long since I've had a vacation, and now that I'm in wolf-mode, practical Zoe has left the vehicle.

"Wow," Mike pretends to be surprised. "When I signed up to drive for Uber, I had no *idea* I'd have such friendly passengers..."

This is a game we play sometimes; that we're strangers who are just meeting.

"You're about to get a five star review..."

"Jesus, Zoe, the road—"

"It's your fault for bringing me into the wild," I tease him, still thinking about what it would feel like to be a wolf, with no one to answer to except the forest herself. The wind whips through my open window, and I turn my attention away from Mike's neck and back to the vast landscape outside. This time I lean even further into the openness, sitting on the edge of the window frame like a bird on a perch, one arm extended wide, invincible.

"Careful," Mike lets his foot off the gas a little, always the more cautious half of our partnership. "And I believe *I* requested a tropical setting," he sighs.

It's true. I forced him to come to Yosemite, and promised we'd do something tropical another time. It was a rare moment for me. Usually I let the other person have their way, no questions asked. But years of therapy in carpeted offices littered with chimes and crystals have made me more mindful of my patterns. When I met Mike, I promised I'd break my bad habits. Apparently, I'm a people-pleaser who "struggles to voice her needs, is habitually distrustful of others, and creates distance as a form of self-protection." It's a nice way of saying that I'm an aloof bitch who copes with fear of abandonment by down-playing her own feelings, desires, and investment in a relationship. People never know where they stand with me.

There's a kind of love story— you've heard it before— where the princess is trapped in a castle, and the prince comes to save her. She knows at once he's the one, and they live happily ever after.

Ours is not that kind of love story.

In our story, Mike is the princess. He is kind, and good, and trusting. Flowers spring up on the grass where he walks. His smile makes the sun shine brighter. Animals gravitate toward him because they can sense the purity of his heart.

Meanwhile, I'm the gnarly ogre who guards the castle

bridge. I question everyone who dares pass, making them answer three riddles before proceeding. If they don't answer correctly, I cast them into the moat, caustic and brittle in my conclusion that they're not to be trusted.

The hotel I work at is my fortress, surrounding my ugliness with beauty, cloaking the worst of me in wrappings so lush my shortcomings are easily overlooked.

When I told Mike about my metaphor for our relationship, I half-expected him to come to his senses and break up with me.

"Don't you see? You fell in love with the ogre when you should've waited for a prince!"

He laughed. "What can I say? The big ears really do it for me."

That's the thing about Mike. He has his own kind of magic. It enables him to look past the external— the thorns and barbs around the flower of a person— straight into the core of who they are. He only sees the best in me.

An alarm blares, taking me by surprise and making my hand slip from the edge of the window. Suddenly, I'm teetering toward the black asphalt, scraping against the car's smooth paint toward oblivion. I'm sure I'm going to fall, but Mike grabs onto the belt loop in my jeans, pulling me back into the car. We weave into the other lane, but there's no oncoming traffic out here in the wilderness. If we were still in Silverlake, we'd be dead.

"You okay?" He asks, a little shaken.

"Yeah," I answer, trying not to let on how close I was to becoming road kill.

There's a moment of silence in which we're both considering the fragility of what's stable, and the nearness of disaster. Then, a silky sound echoes beside me as Mike uses the driver controls to roll-up the passenger-side window.

We lean in to look at Mike's phone— a text message is the source of the alarm bell— strapped to the dashboard in a holder connected to the vents. It's not beeping anymore, but it shakes as the car hits rough asphalt, as if it dreads the name on its screen as much as Mike does:

Cassandra.

Mike groans, "Not again."

"Do you want to read it?"

"No," he hesitates. "Do you?"

It's a rare invitation. Mike is like a piece of sea-glass, multi-faceted and saturated, hard to look away from but still easy to see through. He doesn't keep secrets, and he's an open book about everything in our relationship, except *her*. He's given me the basics: a disgruntled ex who stalks him, new addresses and phone numbers be damned. He's been fair in sharing details, and revealed that he had a stalker as soon as things between us got serious. He said he wanted me to decide if it was something I could live with, and he'd understand if it wasn't. I stayed, but the ogre in me keeps one eye open, looking not at Cassandra, but at Mike.

Strangely, Cassandra herself doesn't bother me. In fact, I think I might like her. The letters she sends, sprayed with perfume, soft and sweet, not so strong as to be cloying. The way she leaves the mail by the door, stacked in order from important to junk. She might lack boundaries, but even in her trespasses, Cassandra tries to be unobtrusive. I've never met her in-person, but her actions describe her character. There's a permanent question in everything she does, like she's walking through life with her hand patiently raised, waiting to be called on by a teacher who's no longer there. It's a side-effect of some deeper phenomenon all women experience, one I can relate to but can't quite put into words. The closest I've come to describing it is that it's like being told you're a brunette, but looking in the mirror and seeing a blonde. It's some fundamental mismatch between who you are, and how others see you, and I know if I met Cassandra— if I mentioned it, even just the start— she'd understand immediately. If she weren't stalking my boyfriend, I'm pretty sure we'd be friends.

No, it's not Cassandra who makes my inner ogre raise the drawbridge. It's Mike, and his refusal to disclose the details of their break up. My ogre doesn't like his answers to my riddles.

"She's sick," is his favorite refrain, his dark eyes webbed with sympathy. "She's not right in the head. One day she'll get help."

He claims he's trying to shield me from something that's "his problem," but his vagueness makes me sure there's more to it. But then I remember that I have eyes coated in doubt, and that I'm always looking for the worst in people, even in the very best of moments. In the comfortable darkness of night, wrapped in sheets we spent too much money on, the TV humming with the evening news— in the seconds before sleep, when any other woman would roll over and tell the man she loves how glad she is to have him, I curl into Mike's arms and ask a wordless question. It's one I can't utter aloud, but can still reach out and touch, passing it between my fingers like a lucky coin I won't get rid of.

Is there a monster in you?

He's done nothing to deserve the question, and I know enough about myself that I'm sure I'd be asking it anyway, even if Cassandra didn't exist. It's occurred to me that I could, one day, stop asking it, but that will be the moment Mike reveals the worst in him. Call me superstitious, but Murphy's Law applies. The night you don't check for monsters under the bed is the night one eats you.

Temporarily invited into Mike and Cassandra's secret world, I pull the phone from its holster. It's a weapon in my hands, explosive and unstable. I type in Mike's lock code. He gave it to me once to check an email and never changed it. Like I said, he's sea-glass. Other guys won't let you see inside a sock drawer, but on date number one, Mike will give you his banking information and mother's telephone number.

"Drove past your office," I read aloud, wondering what Cassandra's voice sounds like and if it's anything like mine. "Didn't see you through the window. Where are you?" The words are followed by a few kissy face emojis. Predictable and a little tacky, but lacking in pretense. That's another thing I like about Cassandra. She's too screwed up to pretend to be anyone other than exactly who she is. I search for Mike's reaction, but for a moment he's an enigma, unreadable. "At least she doesn't know where we are," I prompt.

"That's true," he answers, but the slant in his voice says it doesn't make him feel any better.

He looks like a person who's just run through his high-school hallways naked, only to realize it wasn't a dream after all. I understand why.

Dating in adulthood— when you're past your college freshness, and your stories have grown longer with more cryptic endings— means coming into a relationship with a certain amount of baggage. We all have it. Dusty luggage with too many stickers, corners shredded by conveyor belts, locks that don't work and zippers that get stuck.

At twenty-eight, I've spent well over a decade unpacking some of the worst suitcases you've ever seen, only to repack them again and send their owners to the nearest bus depot.

First there was Dave, who forgot to mention that he'd folded up a wife inside his carry-on. Then there was Aaron, who bundled up a debilitating fear of commitment and placed it in the front pocket of his sensible duffle-bag, to be removed only when two years of energy had been spent "working on the relationship." He got married six months later, unpacking another surprise: he wasn't afraid of commitment. He just didn't love me enough. Last but not least was Jerome, whose baggage was basically just that he was an asshole.

Each of these relationships left its mark on me, until one day I opened up my own suitcase (a wheel-along weekender with very comfortable handles), and found an inability to trust anyone, at all, ever. It was probably always there, hiding under crumbs and receipts, but it doubled in size, and I fed it daily like a beloved pet. It kept me safely alienated from the perils of love for awhile.

Then, I met Mike, and the world rearranged itself.

Falling for him happened entirely by accident. He makes furniture— hand-crafted, beautiful things, built from rare types of woods— the sort of stuff ritzy establishments like my hotel invest in.

The day he walked in to try and sell us on a carved wooden table for the sitting area of the lobby, he brought the piece with him, loaded into the back of a busted old van.

It was so beautiful it made me want to cry. Something about it moved; spiraling legs curved into a textured top, every notch built with care. It was so alive it practically breathed.

On our first date, Mike showed me his workshop. His fingers were stained brown with varnish, and he smelled like oak and sawdust. First, we were casual— my choice, not his. Then, we were something else. My ogre let down the bridge and helped him cross the moat, but my defensive walls remained in place, ready to eject him should he prove to be anyone other than the man he presents. When we moved in together, I insisted that the lease be in my name. Dolly Parton once said the key to a happy relationship is always having a suitcase packed. I go one step further and keep my car keys in the ignition. I'm always searching for fangs in the the mouth of the man I'm with.

That's why when Mike, "needed to tell me something" a few months into our too-good-to-be-true relationship, I wasn't surprised. I waited for him to admit to being a serial killer, or an ex-con, but instead he confessed to having a stalker. He'd met Cassandra in college, and they'd had a five-year relationship before she lost her mind and things went South. It wasn't the worst baggage I'd unpacked. And I could relate to the feeling of discovering the person you thought you knew was a Russian stacking doll all along, hiding multiple versions of himself deep under skin and bone.

Prior to Mike, I'd endured the hell of dating apps, taking a last, half-hearted stab at love by creating a generic bio, throwing up a few pictures of myself at the beach, at work, as a butterfly on Halloween.

Even there— in that digital, surface-level environment consisting of impressions and guesses— I encountered the phenomenon of a human within a human— a social turducken. I chatted for weeks with a guy who seemed completely harmless. His name was "Josh Q.," and his interests included video games, baseball, and hiking. We played a game where we wrote to each other in rhyming stanzas, always increasing the difficulty.

```
"How  was  your  day?  What  happened  at
work?"
    "It  was  great,  how  'bout  yours?  Just
asking  to  lurk."
    "I  didn't  do  much.  Did  you  watch
Game  of  Thrones?"
    "Why  yes,  yes  I  did,  And  my  mind  was
so  blown!"
```

It was a stupid way to trade messages, but the novelty of it caught my attention. We even made plans to meet, but I cancelled when Mike walked into my life, bringing his toffee-colored skin and reassuring smile. No one could compare, and I deleted the app a few days later— but Josh Q. still found me. He added me on Facebook, and followed me on Instagram. When I messaged him to tell him I was seeing someone, his reaction made me wish I hadn't written him at all.

"Would've been nice to know that before I wasted my time. You bitches are all the same." I resisted the temptation to write back in rhyme: "Us bitches are all the same... we think you're really *lame*."

The experience was a warning, a reminder that people can surprise you, no matter how benign they seem on the outside. It was a small drop in a bucket I've been filling since third grade, when my Dad found a family he liked better, and left me and Mom with nothing but one of his old sweatshirts, which we donated to Goodwill. It's the sticky feeling you get when you meet someone new, and you wonder if they're even worth the trouble. It's the hand of an older mentor on your back, placed just low enough to introduce a question. It's the humming undertone during dinner at a friend's house, when you notice your friend's husband gripping his wine glass a little too tightly. People hide the worst of themselves. It's a truth I've accepted— one that Mike will never believe, even as Cassandra hovers in the background of his life, never near enough to see, but always close enough to feel. That's the difference between Mike and me. I've learned that all people are either a predator, or prey. It just takes time to know which one you're dealing with.

Mike pulls the phone from my hands and shoves it in the glove compartment, jolting me back to the present moment.

"Let's not talk about her this week," he mutters as he closes the glove compartment too hard. He rarely gets angry, and the emotion hangs from his shoulders like a suit that's too big. "I just want to be..."

He doesn't finish the thought, but he doesn't have to.

"Free," I add. He nods, pressing on the accelerator so that the pine trees whip past my window, turning the world into a green blur that won't slow down for me, no matter hard I try to blink it into focus.

MORE FROM VALERIE BRANDY

The Annie Hudson Real Estate Mystery Series:

- "Murder Behind the Gates" — The Annie Hudson Real Estate Mystery Series, Book One.
- "Murder in the Penthouse" — The Annie Hudson Real Estate Mystery Series, Book Three.
- "Murder in the Commune" — The Private Annie Hudson Real Estate Mystery Series, Book Four.

The Predator / Prey Thriller Series:

- "Trail of Obsession" — The Predator / Prey Thriller Series, Book One.
- "Lies Run Deep" — The Predator / Prey Thriller Series, Book Two.
- "The Trap is Set" — The Predator / Prey Thriller Series, Book Three.
- "The Woman in the Wind" — The Predator / Prey Thriller Series, Book Four.

COMING SOON:

The Rebecca Orange Cozy Castle Mystery Series

- Mystery at Monrovia Castle — Book One
- A Victim in the Village — Book Two
- A Royal Ruse — Book Three

LETTER FROM THE AUTHOR

Dear Reader,

Thank you for dedicating your time to the Pirvate Investigator Annie Hudson Mystery Series! It's wonderful to be able to speak with you and hear what you want from characters in my novels. This book, in particular, is special to me as Sunray is a real place, and my great-grandmother— Sophia Barnak— really did own a farm and corner store there. My ancestors were responsible for helping to form this real Polish community many years ago.

I hope you'll reach out to me by joining my mailing list at the link below! I love to keep my readers updated on new releases, offer advanced copies, free giveaways of novellas, sneak previews, and more. If you liked Annie Hudson, I hope you'll keep reading the rest of the series, which continues to grow! In addition, my "Predator/ Prey" thriller series is available now in all formats, starting with book one, "Trail of Obsession."

And if you want to read more from me in general, I hope you'll check out the list of my books on the previous page.

Warmly,

Valerie Brandy

Join the Author's Mailing List at:
    www.valeriebrandy.com